# THE DEVIL'S BULLET

## AND OTHER SHORT STORIES
## FROM EXMOOR

# THE DEVIL'S BULLET

## AND OTHER SHORT STORIES
## FROM EXMOOR

BY

# JERRY DAN

Black Lab
Books

First edition published by
Rare Books and Berry, 2008

First re-print, 2009

Published by
Black Lab Books,
Ascot
Berkshire
SL5 8BY

ISBN 978-0-9562356-0-2

Typeset in Minion

Printed in Great Britain by the MPG Books Group,
Bodmin and Kings Lynn

# Contents

# Introduction

EXMOOR never ceases to amaze and encourage. It is full of legend, roaming beasts and houses that lurk in the pits of valleys or nestle along the coastline. For countless generations it has stimulated writers and poets.

Glenthorne is one of the houses, a pile that remains a mystery to this day, evoking tales of German U-boats moored nearby. Wartime establishments on Exmoor that once housed men employed on secret operations are now empty and derelict. Even now, official records of what happened in them remain closed to the general public despite the passing of more than sixty years.

And then there are the people.

The environs of Porlock have long been favoured by those who wish to forget their past, and by many whose lives have involved employment in the most secret spheres of government. 'The Devil's Bullet' is a term that is still used by assassins who work for that most sinister function in the Russian Intelligence Services, the 'Department of Wet Tricks'. Any Russian defector remains forever on the list of targets for such assassins, who operate with a blanket permission to kill. Few defectors are able to live out the rest of their lives in safety.

'The Devil's Bullet' and other stories involve such mysteries and it is up to the reader to gauge the level of truth in each tale. The final story contains no fiction – only true heroism by people who risked their own lives to rescue others. It is an accurate account of an event that took place in 1942 in the marshland of Porlock, this author having located a file in a US military archive. History often requires rewriting as new information and documents shed new light on events.

JERRY DAN
Porlock
December 2008

# Glenthorne

## THE HOUSE OF MYSTERY

BOTH LETTERS had been anonymous. The major in the War Office had merely glanced at the first, just one of hundreds that daily poured into various government departments and Scotland Yard from all over the country with accounts of mysterious encounters, sightings of strangers, overheard conversations in pubs and suspicions regarding neighbours. German infiltrators lurked everywhere according to the diligent and highly watchful public, who were a vital source of intelligence to Special Branch and MI5. This letter had been logged and filed: no action was required. The major saw no reason to send it on to his usual contacts in the overstretched intelligence services.

It was the explosive content of the second letter from the unnamed resident of Porlock in West Somerset that led the major to urgently request a map of the South West of England – one with the largest scale so he could identity the big houses that perch on the rugged coastline of the Bristol Channel between Minehead and Lynmouth.

He needed to locate Glenthorne.

It was late November 1943 and the war was turning for the Allies. Churchill, Roosevelt and Stalin were meeting in Teheran to discuss the strategy for the final victory over Hitler. The Battle of Berlin was in full swing, with almost nightly bombing missions over the German capital by Lancasters and Mosquitoes. 'Bomber' Harris, the chief of Bomber Command, had declared, '*We can wreck Berlin from end to end…*' The Soviet Red Army, revitalised by the success at Stalingrad in February that year, was overwhelming the Wehrmacht and Waffen SS by sheer weight of numbers on many fronts. On the Home Front, Britain had just experienced one of the best harvests ever, a remarkable achievement given that crops had been grown on the smallest acreage of land yet recorded since substantial acreage had been given over to the war effort. Britain's Land Army and the farmers had performed tirelessly.

There was real optimism among the villagers in Porlock that the war would soon be over, and that pre-war tranquillity would return to the community. There had been calls to government from throughout the country that Civil Defence volunteers be released from some of their duties. Minehead attracted cinemagoers in their droves with a raft of new films. Leslie Howard had made his last movie, *The Gentle Sex* – more a dramatised documentary of girls in the ATS – and it was a huge success. Also thrilling the audiences was *Desert Victory*, the story of the advance of Britain's Eighth Army from El Alamein to Tripoli.

Obtaining a travel warrant, the major returned home that evening. In the morning he packed an overnight bag and caught a bus to Paddington. The railways throughout the country were trying their best to provide a service but the schedule was haphazard. Coal for the trains was in very short supply. Ernest Bevin, the Minister of Labour, would shortly be announcing the introduction of the 'Bevin Boys' – young men under the age of 25 who were to be conscripted to serve down the mines. Coal production had slumped alarmingly to 200 million tons in 1943 and the number of miners had fallen to 700,000, even though many miners had returned from the army.

The major caught a train to Reading and waited in the station tea-room for two hours for a connection to Bristol. Another change would take him to Taunton. He had decided against yet another connection to Dulverton. At Taunton the driver he had ordered was waiting.

The major had never been to Exmoor and he revelled in its beauty, so different from the wartime greyness of London. The pale winter sunshine shone through the boughs of the trees, now shorn of their leaves. Sitting back in his car, he asked questions of his driver, a local man who had decided against the main road to Minehead and instead was treating the major to views of Exmoor. At Dunkery the driver stopped and the major alighted to drink in the view. In front of him was the Bristol Channel, with Wales beyond; below lay Porlock. The car struggled in first gear to climb Porlock Hill, which worried the major, but the driver seemed confident they would make it. A short while later the car sped past the Culbone stables, by which time the major was studying his map. They passed County Gate and missed the track 800 yards on the right. They turned around and parked by the post box. The road was deserted. The entrance had no sign. The major checked the map again. Glenthorne must lie at the end of the track, a Victorian mansion situated in glorious isolation, apart from a nearby farmhouse.

He opened his bag, changed out of his uniform and exchanged his shoes for a pair of stout boots. It was difficult to gauge the distance to Glenthorne but he estimated it to be about three miles. Judging from the close contours on the map, it would be a tough and steep descent. He didn't relish the climb back up the valley.

As the driver settled down in his seat for a snooze, the major set off with binoculars in hand. It was cold, the air damp with the winter chill. The major was in a hurry. There were few hours of daylight left. He wasn't far down the winding track when he saw the huge mass of rhododendron bushes – he had never seen so many. They must look magnificent when in bloom, he thought. The track soon wove its way through the thick woods. An hour later he was above Glenthorne.

Despite the fading light he could clearly see the house. Many of the curtains were closed. It looked bleak, somewhat desolate. An elderly man appeared from the back of the house and made his way to the substantial kitchen garden to pick vegetables before returning to the house.

The major scanned the surrounding area. It was clear why the letter writer had wanted anonymity. To have observed what he did, he could only have been a fisherman – not a legal fisherman with a permit but one of a countless number nationwide who took to the

water under cover of night and sold their catch on the flourishing
black market. Several times, the writer said, he had seen the light off-
shore, a swaying light. It appeared to come from the promontory to
the left of the house, the location of the waterfall. The swaying was
a signal to a vessel in the Bristol Channel. The second letter to the
War Office had been even more descriptive. A vessel had been sighted
about ten minutes after the light was extinguished. This wasn't a fishing boat. It was a German U-boat.

The only way that the fisherman who wrote the letter could have observed the subsequent events, surmised the major, would have been if he had rowed his boat onto the shore and hidden. The fisherman had seen a dinghy from the U-boat land on the stony beach in front of Glenthorne, where there was a small jetty. Two men had alighted, speaking softly in German as they made their way up the path, over the front lawn and into the house. Two other dinghies appeared out of the night with six more men, their faces blackened; they all seemed very familiar with the procedure that followed. Within fifteen minutes they had filled their large water canisters from the waterfall and loaded them into the dinghies before disappearing back into the blackness of the Bristol Channel.

With the light now fading fast, the major left his observation spot to return to the car. Rather than taking the winding track he made a decision to shorten the route by going through the woods. He set off at a gentle trot, mulling over in his mind his course of action once back in London. Very quickly into his ascent the hill became steeper, and on reaching a clearing he sat down to rest, breathing deeply. Around him he noticed the variety of tree types: oak, elm, beech and some birch.

At first the noise was almost indiscernible, but then it grew in intensity. The major sat as if bolted into the ground, every hair on his body standing on end. It sounded like rasping air being expelled through the windpipe of an animal. The noise was being emitted to his left, behind some undergrowth, but very quickly the same sound was also to his right.

Very slowly, the major moved his head to the left. What he saw would affect him for the rest of his life. Sitting on its haunches a mere ten yards away was a cat, neither domestic nor feral but a wild beast, huge and inky black. The beast's eyes were staring straight at the intruder in the clearing, its fangs bared. Turning slowly to the right, the major saw the other one, crouched, as if preparing to attack.

Slowly and gently, the major manoeuvred his hand into his bag, slowly grasping the handle of his service revolver and pulling it out. At that very moment the crouched animal raced towards him and

sprang. The major screamed, turned his head and flung himself face-
down onto the ground. Inexplicably, the animal didn't attack. It
merely jumped right over him and joined its mate. Before they disappeared into the wood the major looked up and noticed the tails of

the two animals. They were extraordinarily long, almost dragging along the ground.

Without waiting to see if they were about to return, the major jumped up, and he ran as he had never run before. Somewhere above him, not far away, he could hear shouting. His name was being called. By a stroke of luck he stumbled across the track back to the road. The light had completely gone by the time the major banged on the window of the car. But the car was empty; the driver had gone. That puzzle was soon solved when the driver turned up a few minutes later. Worried about the major, he had ventured a short distance down the track. In the deepening gloom he had veered off into the woods and was momentarily lost, though he soon found his bearings. It was the driver who had shouted the major's name.

The major sat in complete silence, his hands trembling, as they drove to Porlock. He wanted to relate his experience to the driver but was disinclined to do so, in case he was ridiculed. With the car's partly blacked-out headlamps giving barely sufficient light, the driver gingerly negotiated Porlock Hill before stopping outside the Ship Inn. The major got out and requested that he be collected early in the morning for the trip back to the railway station at Taunton.

That evening the major sat in the tiny bar in front of a roaring fire, deep in thought, his mind a maelstrom of the events of the afternoon. The regulars had grown used to military people coming through Porlock for exercises on Exmoor, but this officer, who carried a revolver, made them feel uncomfortable. He had attempted to engage the elderly barman in a conversation over illegal fishing, asking whether it was a common practice in the village. The barman had pretended not to hear, carrying on his conversation with the regulars.

When the major returned to the bar for another pint, he asked the barman whether he had ever been to Glenthorne. A marked hush suddenly descended on the pub, and when the major turned to examine the faces in the room none would hold his gaze. Quickly finishing his drink, he walked over to them – men who had probably fought in the Great War but who were too old for this one.

'Gentlemen,' he asked, 'have there ever been sightings of large animals on Exmoor – in particular large cats?'
As with the mention of Glenthorne, this question was left unanswered, hanging in the smoke-filled atmosphere of the Ship Inn.

*

Within days of the major's return to London, MI5 deployed a team of 'watchers' to Porlock, some of them retired Special Branch officers who mixed freely with the inhabitants of the village, casually sounding out any suspicions regarding Glenthorne. More often than not they were unsuccessful. The very mention of Glenthorne seemed to generate both fascination and unease. Other 'watchers' spent days and nights covertly in the woods near County Gate. By the end of 1943 the U-boats had ceased their visits to Glenthorne. Apart from one.

Given its unique location, MI5 and MI6 began to use the house for private meetings, when the agenda was too secret to be discussed in London. On at least two occasions in 1943 and 1944 Britain engaged in dialogue with Nazi Germany in an attempt to solicit a peace settlement so that they could concentrate on another enemy – Bolshevism. Soviet agents in London stole the details of both efforts and these documents are still kept in a storage box in a disused cell in the Lubyanka. They have never been made public.

Donald Maclean, one of several high-placed Soviet sources in the Foreign Office, had passed the first document to his controller on December 23, 1943. This detailed planned Anglo-German negotiations in Portugal between Winston Churchill and Joachim von Ribbentrop, Hitler's foreign minister. Von Ribbentrop had been Ambassador to Britain from 1936. When he had departed in 1938 he was an Anglophobe.

The second document is dated August 27, 1944, two months after D-Day. Churchill, accompanied only by his private secretary and not by Foreign Secretary Anthony Eden, was received by Pope Pius XII in his private quarters at the Vatican. Later in the day there were discussions with Ernst von Weizsäcker, Germany's Ambassador to the Vatican, and General Walter von Brauchitsch and Field Marshal Wilhelm Keitel, two of Hitler's key military aides. Details of these meetings were made available to the Russians courtesy of 'Scott', the codename of the most senior spy operating within the Foreign Office, whose identity has never been discovered by the British intelligence services. Churchill laid down several conditions if Germany was to surrender. '*The Germans have to co-operate in eliminating the danger of Communism*,' read the final minute in the Lubyanka document.

Increasingly in 1944 Churchill and Roosevelt came to believe that, after they had dealt with Germany and Japan, Joe Stalin would be the new enemy. A peace settlement to shorten the war with Germany was considered a priority. A number of meetings took place on British soil between British and German intelligence officers, sanctioned at the very highest level in both countries.

Did that last U-boat visit to Glenthorne in 1943 herald the beginning of this dialogue? Were those present in the beautiful drawing-room, with its unique curved doors that led out to the hallway and the immaculate lawns, setting the agenda for Churchill and von Ribbentrop in Portugal? Glenthorne will forever hold its secrets.

And the major? After the war he returned to Porlock and visited County Gate. He walked down the path into the woods, looking for the clearing where he had seen the animals, but he never found it. At the Ship Inn the regulars were just as uncommunicative as they had been in 1943.

*

Around 1968 (the actual year is now forgotten), amongst the visitors to Porlock was somebody who wanted to relate a wartime event. He had never been to Porlock before, but he had been near to it. During the war he was an officer in a German U-boat, part of a 'wolf pack' operating in the Atlantic. From time to time his vessel would hug the southern coastline of the Bristol Channel and wait for the light – a swaying light – which would guide them to a waterfall with fresh water for the crew. This was a common occurrence in

1943, he said. His was not the only U-boat that surfaced there for water.

These 'welcomed' guests to the Bristol Channel often had other missions. The U-boats would collect members of the Abwehr, the German organisation responsible for intelligence-gathering and covert operations in enemy territory, from a bay very close to the tiny settlement of Dunquin in south-west Ireland and deliver them to England.

It is known that large animals have lurked in the undergrowth and woodland near County Gate for several generations.

This short story was first published in *The Exmoor Review*, 2006 edition, Vol. 47, pp.61-5.

# Sid

S ID WAS BOTH thief and hero, two attributes he consummated with great skill and cunning. He stole only as a necessity. Later, when a hero, there were few as brave.

Horace, Sid's father, had been a survivor of the Third Battle of Ypres, the Passchendaele offensive. Between July and November 1917, the British, without their French allies, had launched a massive assault on German positions. Passchendaele was a senseless slaughter of a battle and even the war-weary British public, seemingly now impervious to the shocking level of casualties in French and Belgian Flanders, was horrified at the numbers of dead in this latest campaign by Field Marshal Douglas Haig and his army generals.

In common with so many others in the trenches, Horace had fallen victim to the terrible effects of mustard gas. He had been issued with a gas mask after the Germans in April 1915 had for the first time in the war, released chlorine from thousands of cylinders along the trenches occupied by French Territorial and Algerian units in the First Battle of Ypres. At Passchendaele Horace's mask had a fault in the rubber and he immediately succumbed to excruciating pain. The skin on his face felt as if on fire and his eyes streamed. A mate, seeing Horace in distress, slung him over a shoulder and ran with him to a medic station. The Great War had another eleven months to run, but for Horace the war was over. He was invalided back to England and returned to Manchester, the city of his birth. It was a key centre of the British armaments industry and had supplied vast weapon-power for the war.

The ending of the Great War, a European conflagration the cause of which lay mainly in the signing of alliances between the Great

Powers in the early years of the twentieth century, brought new hope and new expectations throughout Europe and Britain. A month after Germany signed the Armistice in November 1918, accepting blame for the war, the British Prime Minister Lloyd George and his coalition government sought a fresh public mandate. Lloyd George's resounding victory in the first General Election in which women were allowed to vote was won by focusing on reconstruction and the creation of a country 'fit for heroes to live in'.

To Horace, and tens of thousands of other ex-servicemen, these were idle promises of a utopia that would bypass the medically unfit. Industry had shifted its priorities from munitions manufacture to fulfilling new post-war demands. New skills were called for. Labour became competitive. Men returned from war only to find their places on the factory floor occupied by women, the same women who had put fuses into artillery shells and drilled out gun barrels. Horace could find only menial employment. Often he had to take time off, without pay, as he experienced uncontrollable spasms of coughing, sometimes bringing up blood. The gas he had inhaled at Passchendaele had forever scarred his lungs.

He met Betty, a cook, in one of the factories where he worked, and together they moved into a single room. They soon married, and lived in abject poverty.

At one job interview, when his coughing was exceptionally bad, the interviewer suggested that Horace should move to the country to improve his health. Horace had heard of Exmoor from a friend, who had never visited it but imagined that the air was pure and the running water sweet. Betty was worried when Horace first mentioned a move. She was the regular breadwinner in the relationship, though her wage as a cook was pitiful. But she knew that Horace would not live long if they remained in urban Manchester. It was with the greatest apprehension that they caught a train south to begin a new life.

*

They had forsaken one squalid room in Manchester for similar squalor in Dulverton. Betty found some shop work but Horace found nothing. The skills he had demonstrated on a factory floor were in no demand in rural Exmoor. Horace was in despair.

It was Betty who heard about the positions. During her short lunch-break she ran home to tell her husband. The following day Betty quit her job and they set off for Molland, cadging a lift from a Dulverton grocer making deliveries. In the back of the grocer's cart Horace prayed that they were not too late. The possibility of regular employment was too good to miss.

A dog barked from within the great barn at the noise of the large farm gate being opened. Within moments two dogs appeared, their fangs bared to greet the uninvited guests. Horace was terrified and Betty froze, dropping her bag of belongings. A man appeared from the barn and whistled. The dogs obeyed and sat on their haunches, eying the two intruders.

'What do you want here?' boomed the farmer.

'We've come about the positions, sir. We're from Dulverton. I can work and my wife can cook.' Horace tried to regain some measure of composure. 'I'll work whatever hours are necessary, sir, mark my words. That's a promise,' he added quickly.

'Come inside,' said the farmer, after what seemed an age.

He offered them tea, making it himself. There was no sign of a woman in the house. The scullery appeared unkempt and in need of cleaning.

Horace wanted to start the conversation but felt he shouldn't. Betty sat in a chair staring down at her feet, embarrassed by the situation.

'You can cook?' enquired the farmer of Betty.

'Yes, sir.' Her response was barely audible. 'I can also clean.'

'And you?'

Horace had dreaded this question. He had been churning over in his mind whether to lie or confess that he had never worked on the land.

The farmer sensed the hesitation. 'Did you fight?'

'Yes, sir, and proud of it too, I was.' Horace cheered up. There was now hope. 'I was an enlisted man. Signed up with my mate Tommy, I did, sir, in the 6th Battalion of the Manchester Regiment in August

1914. We were the first in the queue, we were, so proud to wear our caps with the Manchester tram badge. Tommy died in our first engagement in France, shot through the head he was, by a sniper. We were in the trench, having a smoke, waiting. Tommy lifted his head. He dropped down dead at my feet, a bullet right in his forehead. I'll never forget it.'

'Were you at the Somme?'

'I was, sir, and bloody carnage it was too.'

'And Passchendaele?'

'I was there too, sir. By Passchendaele all the mates I'd enlisted with were dead. Many of them literally blown to bits, sir, right in front of my eyes. I was lucky,' he said with bitterness in his voice. 'There was not much left of the 6th Battalion by April 1918 and it was disbanded in July.' Horace felt guilty that he hadn't admitted to being invalided out of the army in 1917.

The farmer sat back in his chair and finished his tea. An awkward silence pervaded the room. Betty stared at the floorboards, certain that they would be asked to leave. She saw the rejection on Horace's face, a look she had witnessed many times in Manchester.

Deep in thought, the farmer got out of his chair, placed his empty cup in the filthy sink and moved over to the window to stare out at the evening gloom and mist descending on the moor. He, too, had stark memories of war.

'In the South African War I was wounded at Spion Kop, shot in the arm by a Boer marksman,' he said quietly. 'We lost almost the entire regiment. Only a few of us escaped with our lives, leaving our dead behind. God it was hot – it was the middle of an African summer. We came home, but there was no welcome for heroes. The newspapers said the war was a failure, despite our final victory over Kruger. The Boer won the sympathy not the poor bloody foot-soldier who dragged his arse across the veldt to fight an invisible army. The Boer was a canny soldier.'

A new atmosphere enveloped the room, one of mutual respect. The two veterans recalled past battles and lost comrades. But reality quickly returned.

'You have no experience as a farm labourer,' said the farmer, not as a question but as a statement.

'No, sir, none.'

The farmer contemplated for a while his clutter and the thick dust that had accumulated on the furniture since his wife had passed away.

'You have the job, and your wife, too.'

Horace beamed and shook the farmer's outstretched hand. Betty smiled, inwardly ecstatic.

'Thank you, sir, Betty and I will serve you well.'

They moved into a dilapidated tied cottage in a nearby field, rent free. Betty soon cleaned it and turned it into a home, even with the barest of furniture. In the following months Horace took to the roof to replace the thatch, and quickly mastered the skill. He revelled in the fresh air of Exmoor and became accomplished in all the tasks set him by the farmer.

Sid was born there.

*

It was clear to everyone that Horace's health was failing. The awful cough had returned and for days on end he took to his bed. The doctor from North Molton was familiar with the symptoms: there were others like Horace whose strength was fading away as their lungs deteriorated. Sid took over his father's duties on the farm; his mother had reluctantly given up cleaning and cooking for the farmer to nurse Horace. The farmer showed every consideration and from time to time would allow Sid to slaughter a lamb for food. Betty would profusely thank the farmer for his kindness.

There were medicines available that would help alleviate Horace's condition, but they were expensive. Sid could see that his beloved father was suffering.

At a very early age Sid had explored Exmoor. When he was five his mother had found him, after he had gone missing, attempting to round up sheep. As the years went on, when the days lengthened in the summer he would help his father after school and then slip out of the back door of the cottage onto the moor. For hours he would roam the woods, watch the deer and learn how to forage. Often he would return home and place a dead rabbit on the kitchen table for his mother to skin. His parents never complained about their son's disappearances – they knew he would always return. There were times when Sid slept in the woods, building himself dens that the most adventurous Exmoor walker and farmer would never discover. Sid was learning the survival skills that would later save his life.

At school Sid sat as far away from the teacher as he could. He wasn't bright, but neither was he stupid as the teacher often implied. He was short in height compared to some in the class, but he was muscular, with powerful forearms thanks to the forking and lifting of bales of hay on the farm. Sid certainly knew how to look after himself, as two school bullies learnt to their cost. For a number of years these boys had terrorised others after class, careful to use their fists away from the school playground and the eyes of the teachers.

The day Sid's best friend was set upon was the day Sid reacted. Sid was 14. It was his last year at school.

The bullies never heard Sid approach them from behind as they swaggered home from school. Powerful hands pulled them into the bushes. He kneed one in the crutch and grabbed an arm of the other, twisting it high behind the back. Both collapsed to the ground, writhing in agony, their cloak of invincibility in shreds. Sid slowly extracted his hunting knife from his rucksack and ran his fingers down the large blade. The bullies screamed and their eyes bulged in panic.

Sid had no intention of using his knife, of course. Instead, he said something to them, and watched with satisfaction as the colour they had left in their faces finally drained away. The following day two boys walked through the school gates, no longer displaying their usual boastfulness and arrogance. They looked glum. To those they had hurt over the weeks and months they reluctantly offered their apologies, under the watchful eye of Sid.

Within the day Sid's actions were the talk of the school. They soon reached the ears of Sid's teacher, who felt he should investigate. The bullies were interviewed but they declined to provide any answers.

There was no punishment for Sid, only a smile of appreciation from the teacher.

Poor working class kids left school at 14 in those days. On Exmoor there were no apprenticeships. Only hard work on the land beckoned. The farmer paid Sid a small wage to help his father, who was already struggling. The cough had returned, and was growing progressively worse. Money was tight but there was sufficient to put food on the plate and to buy some clothes. Betty baked cakes for richer families in the village. When Horace's health deteriorated and the doctor confined him to bed the household income collapsed and there was no money to buy medicines to alleviate the coughing spasms.

Reluctantly Sid embarked on the only course of action that seemed open to him. He began to thieve. At night he stealthily crossed the moorland to outlying farms distant from Molland. Stealing from strangers lessened his deep feelings of guilt.

No one ever heard Sid as he broke into their home. He knew how to confront household pets; he had a way of turning them into silent friends. He took nothing but money, aware that it was usually left in a jug or an old tin. Before the sun came up Sid would be home with his loot and a rabbit. He would leave his pickings on the kitchen table for his mother for the purchase of medicine. She never questioned the source.

The high levels of burglary concerned the police. They questioned local suspects, unaware that the real culprit lived miles away. Sid read the newspaper reports about unsolved crimes but his remorse disappeared when it seemed the medicine for his father was working.

Then Horace died one morning in the summer of 1937.

Sid could see that it would be a beautiful morning as he emerged from the woods and trotted to his home. He hadn't thieved that night. It had been so warm that he had decided to sleep out in a den, to be entertained by a herd of deer. To the stags Sid was never considered the enemy; he was a friend. As soon as he walked through the back door he sensed something was wrong, very wrong. The jug of milk and chunk of bread usually left by his mother for him on his return were absent.

Cautiously Sid walked into the front room. Sometimes he would find his mother there, fast asleep in her usual chair, too tired to drag herself to bed after spending hours looking after her husband. Sid climbed the stairs. The door of his parents' room was open and he could see his mother, silent tears running down her cheeks, holding his father's lifeless hand. She did not hear Sid enter the room to place his hand over hers. Horace looked peaceful. He would now rejoin his old comrades. He would have plenty to tell them, especially Tommy.

*

Sid insisted on digging the grave himself, spurning the services of the church gravedigger. There were many mourners from the village, all keen to pay their respects to an old soldier who had survived the horrors of the Somme and Passchendaele. Betty was pleased to see the doctor had come, as had the farmer who had given her and Horace a job some fifteen years earlier. The gravestone was simple, like the simple man Horace had been all his life. The village stonemason had cut the stone without charge, a kindly act he did for anyone who had come through the Great War. Sid was a pallbearer. The vicar conducted the service, quietly informing the congregation of Horace's wartime contribution and the human sacrifice made by his generation.

Before the coffin was lowered into the grave Sid placed his father's army pay book on the wreath of flowers. His mother gently laid down the cap, the beret of the Manchester Regiment with the cap badge beautifully shined, the Manchester tram gleaming in the Exmoor sun.

For days Sid left the cottage only to attend to his regular work on the farm. In the evenings he sat morosely in his room, looking at the woods and the moor beyond, mourning a father. Downstairs, his mother grieved for a husband.

A conversation with the farmer added to their misery. Sid's wage would have to be reduced as agricultural prices were in decline, said the farmer with genuine sadness in his voice. Sid tried to find extra

work but to no avail. There were some weeks when no money at all came into the house. The balmy summer deteriorated into a wet autumn and a hard winter. The economic mood never lifted.

More bad news was to follow. His mother never complained, but Sid could see that her dress hung limp on her body and her face had grown gaunt. The doctor called several times and finally confided to Sid that she had a debilitating illness which would prove to be terminal. Her life expectancy was uncertain. There were of course drugs, explained the doctor, which could help with the pain …

That night Sid took again to the moor, his clandestine activities resumed. At the farm near Withypool, as in the past, no one heard Sid enter or leave. The following day Sid went to see the doctor and handed over the money. He beamed when he saw the pain ease from his mother's face as the drugs took effect, albeit temporarily.

Over the next week Sid ventured out several times, returning exhausted after tramping through deep snow. He used the woods where he was able to disguise his tracks. One night the snow fell so heavily he slept out, in one of his dens.

Opportunism was Sid's downfall.

He had walked past the large house in Molland many times, never giving it a backward glance. He had never thieved locally – but the front door, slightly ajar, was too tempting. He looked quickly up and down the main street. The village was deathly silent under its covering of snow. Sid gently prised the door open and saw the old woman fast asleep in her chair by the fire. She had obviously forgotten to latch the door properly. Silently, he crossed the room to the dresser and checked the drawers. He stared at the two bundles of money, the savings of a kindly old dear who had lived in the village all her life.

He stood there, the money in his hands. The room was warm and snug, the flickering flames from the fire bouncing shadows off the walls.

Suddenly he had a sense of foreboding. He returned the money to the drawer, turned slowly around and saw recognition in the now wide-open eyes of the old woman. She didn't shout but her darting eyes followed Sid as he made a swift exit.

The game was up. Ahead lay jail – probably Dartmoor. As he ran back home his mind was in turmoil.

Sid's mother was in the kitchen when he ran in, breathless. He immediately confessed to his crimes and was taken aback when she showed no reaction. Tears then ran down her cheeks as she embraced

Sid and told him of her past suspicions. Through her tears she begged him to get away, to escape. Sid felt only shame. His mother would now have to share that shame, publicly, as her life ebbed away, as the cancer continued its terminal spread.

Sid left the house, a home which had harboured much hope and love, and knew he would never see his mother again. The sight of her frail figure framed in the doorway would haunt him for the rest of his life. Her life was at an end, she had told him – soon she would be joining her beloved Horace – but Sid had to start a new life, out of reach of those who would surely come after him. She had quickly packed him some food and spare warm clothes.

He saw the two policemen approaching in the distance as he slipped away. He might stand a chance if he stayed off the roads. Once he was in the woods the trees would be his camouflage, his protection.

Sid was now a fugitive.

⋆

Aim for Bristol docks, his mother had said. Find a ship. That was good advice. He signed up for the first ship that would take him on as crew. It was bound for Hong Kong, via Cape Town and other ports in countries that seemed so distant. The captain was short of a deck-hand and Sid looked a capable replacement to complement the all-Chinese deckhand crew.

With a day to go before sailing, Sid set to work with gusto, impressing everyone. That night he shared an evening with old seadogs from the boiler-room; he revelled and laughed at their stories. Sid had no money to pay for beer, but that was no matter. They had warmed to him. He would soon become a mate. Sid would also develop a strong bond with the Chinese crew members.

He told no one that he was escaping from the law but in Molland matters were taking an unforeseen turn. To protect Betty from the shame of harbouring a thief, the doctor and the farmer informed the police that they would repay all the money that Sid had stolen over the years. With other more urgent matters to attend to, the police accepted the offer and took no further action. When the villagers learned that Sid had stolen solely to provide medicines for his parents, Betty encountered only sympathy and compassion. As villagers do when one in their midst needs help, they rallied around so that Betty could live out her final days surrounded by the warmth and succour of those who knew her.

Several weeks after he had fled, Sid arrived in Cape Town. The entire crew had gathered on deck to see Table Mountain as the freighter approached the busy harbour. After the cargo was unloaded, and new cargo loaded, they were given a few hours shore leave to visit the notorious bars in Dock Road. They set sail at midnight and as the ship steered into deep water the lights from the wooden bungalows that dotted the Clifton coastline glinted through the darkness. More cargo was loaded at Lorenço Marques, their next stop.

Several weeks later they arrived in Hong Kong. Sid was overawed at the array of Chinese junks, colourfully decked with lanterns and drapes, that greeted the new arrival in the harbour.

The captain had already sounded out Sid's plans and offered him the return trip with higher wages. Sid thanked the captain but declined. He must remain a fugitive. After being paid off, he found a bar in Kowloon and contemplated his options. An Australian came over, beer in hand, and introduced himself as Arthur. They were to become good friends.

Hong Kong was a maelstrom of nationalities, crowded with refugees from events in the north. The Japanese army had occupied Manchuria, brutally suppressing all Chinese opposition. In other Chinese provinces civil war raged between communists led by Mao and nationalists commanded by Chiang Kai-shek. In the bars and dives of Hong Kong the talk was of war as Japan continued to arm its colossal war machine. The wealth of the Pacific was in its sights.

Arthur had heard that Nippon Sangyo Gomu KK, the large Japanese rubber plantation concern, wanted to increase its operations in Sabah in north Borneo. Malaya was vital to world oil supplies, accounting for 72 percent of total production. The company, which had 18,000 acres of rubber cultivation throughout Malaya, was recruiting foremen to run its Chinese and Malay labour groups, said Arthur, and the pay on offer was very attractive.

Within the week Sid and Arthur found themselves on a Japanese freighter bound for the port of Sandakan. On their arrival they were driven south on atrocious roads to the coastal town of Tawau on the north-eastern shore of Cowie Harbour, an inlet of the Celebes Sea. For decades Tawau had been renowned as a centre for smuggling by Philippino pirates. It looked run down and oppressive in the over-whelming heat as Sid and Arthur arrived. A none-to-welcoming Japanese manager pointed them in the direction of their living accommodation. That night they found a bar, a squalid fleapit, and laughed when Arthur ventured that Tawau may not have been one of his best suggestions.

It was clear that the Japanese were a major influence in the town. They had their own shops and two Japanese banks, and socialised only amongst themselves. The non-Japanese foremen were treated with indifference, and the Chinese and Malay labour gangs were despised as racially and socially inferior. Each week a steamer arrived in Tawau from Tokyo with provisions and more Japanese, who were clearly not employed by Japanese firms in the town. They had other reasons to visit Tawau. Rubber was loaded for their return trip.

Sid and his Australian mate soon mastered the methods of run-ning a successful rubber plantation, but they found the worsening attitude of the Japanese towards the Chinese disturbing. As foremen, however, they kept their counsel. By the summer of 1939 war clouds loomed in Europe and Sid was keen to return to England to enlist. But Arthur persuaded him otherwise, and Sid reluctantly accepted the advice.

Because of the impending war, the Japanese in Tawau now treated all foreigners with suspicion. Whenever the foreigners, mainly British and Australians, met publicly they did so in the knowledge that there were undoubtedly suspicious eavesdroppers nearby. The news that Germany had invaded Poland provoked jubilation and despair. The Japanese cheered and hung out banners, offering their full support to Hitler. The foreigners could only look on, deeply troubled. There was now a charged atmosphere in the town and in the rubber plant-ations. Some of the foreigners left. Others, like Sid and Arthur, accepted their wages and stayed put in the hope that Europe might come up with a solution other than war.

Their optimism ebbed away as Germany's ambitions accelerated. Sid was now determined to fight, whatever the consequences because of his past, but it was clear that getting back to England would be fraught with difficulty. His frustration increased as he observed the rapid growth of trade between Tawau and Tokyo. The harbour filled with Japanese ships and rubber exports increased. On the plantations the foreman were told that productivity must be doubled.

By the time Germany invaded Russia and the Ukraine in June 1941, living conditions in Tawau had deteriorated to a level many foreigners found unacceptable, given their previous living standards. Luxury items had long vanished from the stores and fuel was rationed. In Sandakan, the centre of administration for Borneo, the British could only wait. They had received reports from London that the Japanese might soon be in the war – but when was unclear.

After the Japanese attack on Pearl Harbor, on December 7, 1941, the foreigners in Borneo came to the stark realisation that the Japanese military and navy would now move to shore up vital raw material supplies.

The first invasion of Borneo took place on the South China Sea coast in the first week of January 1942. There was little or no oppos-ition. The British administration had long realised that to fight with a meagre reservist force would be futile; it would lead to unnecessary casualties. This was an unpopular policy amongst many inhabitants who were prepared to fight. Jesselton was taken on January 9, the Japanese hastily renaming it Api. It was ten days later that Sandakan, on the other side of the island, was taken and renamed Elopura.

The foreigners in Sandakan felt hopeless and abandoned. At first the Japanese commanders were courteous but, as accommodation and essential food supplies were requisitioned for the troops, the mood turned ugly. Troops had yet to appear in Tawau, some hun-dred miles to the south.

Sid, in Tawau, heard that his company had compiled post-invasion plans, which explained the increased number of Japanese in the town. The names of all foreigners in the area, and Chinese plantation workers, were already on lists that would be provided to the Japanese commander when he arrived. In effect, Nippon Sangyo Gomu for some time had been running an undercover fifth-column. The foreigners met covertly to consider their options. The consensus was to wait, in the hope that invasion might not lead to internment. With what he had seen in the rubber plantation of how the Chinese were treated, Sid had a different point of view. He expected the worst.

Sid wasn't on the plantation the day the military arrived. The convoy arrived at midday in the main street and was greeted by the Japanese managers of his company. They bowed low, acknowledging the status of the Japanese commander. Sid waited in the shadows of a building as long as he dared, then raced to the plantation to find Arthur, only to discover that his company had placed armed roadblocks on every road leading out of the town. Deeply worried, he returned to his billet.

For Sid the idea of internment was unacceptable. Even worse, rumours were already circulating in Tawau that some British and Australians in Sandakan had disappeared. He carefully packed a rucksack and climbed out the rear window, narrowly avoiding the platoon of Japanese soldiers that had piled out of a truck on the road in front to arrest him. Within moments, Sid was under the protection of the dense jungle. The skills honed on Exmoor were to be put to a new and deadly test.

Yet again, Sid was a fugitive.

*

At nightfall he crept back into the town and saw a large group of foreigners, including Arthur, sitting in the main street, surrounded by armed guards. Sid slipped back into the jungle but ventured out the following day and saw a camp under construction. The foreigners had spent the night in the open. Of the Chinese labourers there was no sign.

Over the next week Sid monitored the activity in Tawau. The camp for the foreigners had been completed, as had another, nearer the plantation and even more basic, for the Chinese labourers. Each day both groups would be marched under heavy guard to the plantation. In the heat of the day the work was relentless and frenzied. The shirkers were beaten; the weak, who had lost the will to carry on, had their skulls smashed in with rifle butts by the guards.

The beheadings had also begun.

Concealed in the undergrowth, Sid felt sick to his stomach as he watched a group of Chinese being led to a clearing and forced to dig a trench. The six knelt in front of the trench as the Japanese officer swung his samurai sword with deadly effect. After the second time, the officer paused and lit a cigarette before continuing his task, which by his laughter he found amusing. Heads and torsos tumbled into the trench.

Sid withdrew to his jungle den. There he collapsed and fell into a disturbed sleep.

Soon after this terrible episode Sid made contact with the North Borneo guerrillas, a band of mainly Chinese refugees who had fled into the jungle. They had some guns, but were armed mainly with pangas and spears of sharpened bamboo. There was no road in the interior between Sandakan and Jesselton. When the military tried to cross the area they found themselves totally unprepared for the savage conditions. The guerrillas attacked them and none was spared. By the time a larger detachment was sent to flush out the perpetrators, the guerrillas had melted away. During their occupation of Borneo the Japanese never mastered the jungle with its mangrove swamps. The troops had not been trained for jungle warfare. To compensate, the Japanese commander quickly increased the number of troops under his control to 25,000.

Sid did not join in these guerrilla raids. His resistance was to follow a different, a more personal path.

He continued to monitor the activity in Tawau and on the plantation. Sometimes he ventured over to the other side of the island, to Jesselton, where there were a number of dens he could use, all very well hidden from prying eyes. Finding food was never a problem: he lived off the game he caught, and water was abundant. When on his travels he saw or heard Japanese troops he could easily avoid them. They preferred the well-trodden routes.

Sid was becoming increasingly alarmed at the deteriorating condition of Arthur, who appeared emaciated, his body bruised from beatings. But at least he hadn't been taken by the Kempeitai, the dreaded Japanese military police, whose torture methods were on par with those of the German Gestapo. These murderers in uniform had commandeered a building in every town and large village in Borneo for their activities. By September 1943 terror prevailed throughout Borneo, with public executions to discourage resistance. Homes were torched with their occupants barricaded inside. It was the Chinese who bore the brunt of the brutality, but in the PoW camp at Sandakan foreigners died from maltreatment, hard labour and disease. Death stalked Borneo, a land rich in beauty and famed for the courteousness of its native peoples. Rubber production was the overwhelming priority of the Japanese invaders.

In Tawau Sid's frustration and impatience finally came to a head, just as they had outside his school in Molland years earlier.

From his viewpoint overlooking the plantation, Sid watched the antics of a Japanese officer who sauntered along the lines of workers, whipping anyone who dared to look at him. This wasn't the usual procedure at morning roll-call. Three prisoners were pushed out in front and ordered to kneel, but the officer wasn't finished. Arthur, tall and gaunt, stood out in the back line. The officer pointed and two guards pulled Arthur forward to join the other three. The four were lashed and as they fell forwards their heads were pulled back and they were lashed again.

Outrage built up inside Sid.

The four were finally roped together and pulled to their feet. Two guards dragged them off the plantation and the officer strolled disinterestedly behind as the jungle enclosed the group. Eventually he pointed to a clearing next to a mangrove swamp. The guards lined up the prisoners and yelled at them in Japanese to kneel. The officer and the guards then retired to the soft ground for a smoke, blowing smoke rings and laughing as the prisoners knelt under the burning sun. The officer was the first. He never heard behind him the demonic figure with blackened face and beard, long hair tied back, who dealt him a swift killing blow with his hunting knife. The two guards would fare no better. They, too, silently slumped to the ground. Unaware of what was happening behind them, the prisoners continued to kneel. Sid approached them and, through clenched teeth, told them not to make a sound. Arthur recognised the voice of his mate and turned to watch Sid tip the bodies into the reeds of the swamp. Only the crocodiles would find them.

Even in their poor state the prisoners tried to hug their rescuer but Sid urged immediate haste. Over the following week he led the group deep into the interior, to the safety of the Muruts, a tribe Sid had befriended. In early colonial days the Muruts had been cannibals; now they were at peace with their neighbours but were fiercely anti-Japanese. The four Australians remained with the Muruts until liberation.

Sid went on to undertake more rescues. Despite intensive efforts and a huge price on his head, the Kempeitai could never find him. In the PoW and labour camps in Sabah Sid's reported exploits provided hope.

Sid participated in the rising against the Japanese on the night of October 9, 1943, the eve of the great Chinese festival of the Double Tenth, providing intelligence on Japanese military movements. Led by Lt. Albert Kwok, a Chinese who had made contact with the Americans on the Philippines and brought in guns, the uprising was to be a catastrophic disaster. Initially, however, Kwok and his Kinabulu guerrillas succeeded in wiping out garrisons in and around Jesselton. The following morning the Sabah Jack (the North Borneo Union Jack), the flag of China and the Stars and Stripes were triumphantly displayed in the town. The people came on to the streets and cheered their liberation.

Such joy was short-lived. Japanese reinforcements systematically
ransacked and emptied the coastal villages north of Jesselton, exe-
cuting their inhabitants, including women and children. To prevent
further bloodshed, Kwok and his guerrillas surrendered. They were
taken to Jesselton Sports Centre, the Kempeitai torture chamber,
before being sent to the notorious Batu Tiga prison close by. Mercy

was something the Japanese military never contemplated, and on January 24, 1944 the captured guerrillas were taken to Petagas, near the airfield in Jesselton, for public execution. A Japanese cameraman took photographs of Kwok and his key lieutenants lined up and then kneeling, ready for beheading. Some time later the massacre was over: 176 guerrillas had been beheaded or otherwise executed; their bodies were buried in a large trench at the site.

Kwok's revolt had caused consternation among the Japanese. The overall commander in Borneo moved his headquarters from Kuching in Sarawak to Jesselton. By June it was clear that the tide of war in the Pacific was changing. The Japanese were losing to the Allies in many theatres, and their naval fleets were being annihilated. In Borneo the once mighty army starved as supplies from Japan dwindled to a trickle. Cannibalism was rife amongst the soldiers in Borneo, as it was elsewhere. Sid and his Muruti friends, at great risk, tried to alleviate the starvation at some of the camps by leaving food at selected sites for the prisoners.

To everyone's despair the war moved into another year. Conditions were now even more appalling and barbarous. In January 1945 the Japanese commander ordered a jungle death-march of PoWs from Sandakan into the interior, to Ranau, in peace-time a small village on the jungle route from Sandakan to Jesselton but now garrisoned. He hoped there would be no survivors. To his chagrin some did survive the arduous ordeal.

Aerial bombing had now begun and the American and British liberators unleashed enormous devastation below, not just amongst the Japanese. Many Malays died in these attacks and by March only three buildings in Jesselton were left unscathed by the incendiaries. Two further death-marches to Ranau took place but the Muruts, with Sid among them, rescued a number of prisoners and spirited them away.

In June the Australians landed and a bloody fight followed. The Australians did take prisoners but eyes were diplomatically averted when instant and permanent retribution was preferred. After the dropping of the atomic bomb in August 1945, a force of 6,000

Japanese troops marched from Pensiangan to Kenigau to surrender. During the length of the 214-mile walk they were harried and hunted down by the Muruts, who now exacted bloody revenge for four years of grotesque cruelty and carnage.

*

Upon liberation, Sid led his charges out of the jungle. Altogether he and the Muruts had rescued forty prisoners, many from certain death at the hands of the Japanese. The bedraggled group trudged into Sandakan, where they were greeted with total surprise by the senior Australian officer. It was Arthur who spoke for them all and who told the officer about Sid's extraordinary exploits. Sid allowed his Australian friend to do all the talking.

That night Sid was the toast of Sandakan. In the bar, ever modest, he accepted the free beer and slaps on the back but played down his heroism. Arthur vividly described to the Australian troops how Sid had done away with the Japanese officer and two guards to prevent his beheading. A sergeant informed Sid that a Kempeitai officer who spoke English had been captured but was proving unco-operative, especially over the disappearance of the many Chinese inhabitants of Sandakan.

Sid asked a favour.

The following morning he opened the door of the guard-house and the guard, primed by the sergeant, left to have a cup of tea and a smoke. The officer, arrogant even in defeat, was typical of the Japanese military police who had so brutalised Borneo since the invasion. He glowered at the long-haired Englishman, then sneered. He remained sitting.

'Why do you people despise the Chinese?' Sid asked, ignoring the provocation.

The officer spat on the floor.

'Did you keep a count of the people you beheaded?'

This time the officer laughed mockingly at his latest interrogator. He spat again, this time in Sid's face.

Sid grimaced and wiped off the mess. 'Now that was a really bad move', hissed Sid, his face contorted with anger. 'Do you know who I am?'

The Kempeitai officer looked searchingly at the weather-beaten face. 'You stink,' he said flatly, and spat at him again.

'Let me assist you,' posed Sid, this time ignoring the mess dribbling down his cheek. He bent lower to whisper into the officer's ear, then stepped back gleefully to observe his terror. 'I hate bullies,' snarled Sid as he suddenly kicked the stool away. 'Always did.'

The stunned officer lay on the ground, shaking. He had wet himself. Sid callously withdrew his long Exmoor hunting knife from his rucksack, testing the sharpness of its blade with his thumb. In a thrice he viciously yanked the trembling Kempeitai officer up from the floor, sat him back on his stool and, in slow motion, glided the blade over the officer's chest before letting it hover over the heart. This time Sid didn't mince his words.

As Sid closed the door behind him he met the returning guard and the sergeant who had come running at the stomach-churning screams.

'He'll tell you everything you want to know,' said the triumphant Sid to the apprehensive Australians. 'And I didn't lay a finger on him. Honest.'

'What did he say?' the sergeant solicited.

'That I stank,' laughed Sid.

They watched open-mouthed as Sid sauntered away.

*

It was an emotional parting in Sandakan as a tearful Arthur waited to be evacuated aboard a hospital ship bound for Darwin. In the preceding days he had begged a now shaven Sid to join him in Australia, to begin a new life. Arthur was persuasive, but Sid declined. For a while Arthur had believed that Sid would return to Exmoor, a land he and his parents had loved, give himself up and do his time for past crimes. On the busy quayside, surrounded by stretchers being carried aboard, Sid finally shared with Arthur his own destination, and Arthur smiled.

Within weeks the national newspapers of Australia took up the story of how a brave Englishman had, against tremendous odds, rescued Australians and men of other nationalities from death in the Borneo jungles. Newspapers in Britain did likewise and there were recommendations for official recognition of Sid's bravery. No one in Molland told the eager, prying reporters about Sid's past. They, too, were immensely proud.

Sid, however, was not to be found. Once again he had gone to ground. Arthur knew where, but it was a secret he would never share.

For a number of years reports emerged of an Englishman still living in the jungles of Borneo. One sighting had Sid dancing a war dance of the Muruts, lithely stepping between large bamboo poles being banged together by warriors, the tempo increasing to a stunning crescendo. This dance is a fantastic spectacle to anyone who has witnessed it. Another report observed a long-haired foreigner squatting in a jungle clearing, quietly observing a family of playful orangutans. There was an unsubstantiated report that Sid had returned to Exmoor, somewhere, and was living incognito.

In 1950 the Molland village doctor, now retired, received a long-distance phone call. The doctor imparted the news that Betty had passed away in 1939, the pain of her final months made bearable by drugs paid for by his own practice. The caller asked a favour of the doctor – and right up to the doctor's own death flowers were placed once a year on the graves of Horace and Betty, accompanied by an unsigned message.

Sid had been a thief, but he had become a selfless hero. Each year, and for many years, the Australians who Sid had saved gathered to celebrate the man from a moorland in a distant country where the air was crisp and the running water sweet – exactly as Sid had described it in their jungle hideaway.

A memorial garden was erected in 1948 in Sandakan to the memory of the 1,800 Australian and 600 British who perished in the PoW camps and in the three death marches from Sandakan to Ranau. It also commemorates the large number of Malays, Chinese and Muruts who died.

In Petagas, a poignant memorial is placed on the actual site where 176 Kinabulu guerrillas were massacred. Few people now visit this site...more should.

Jesselton would become Kota Kinabulu.

# The Devil's Bullet*

H E KNEW *they* would come. So far he had been lucky, but now the resignation of Harold Wilson as Britain's Prime Minister had finally consigned him to death.

It was a typical Exmoor spring. In March 1976 the grazing fields around Porlock had never looked so lush and green. The long-range forecast pointed to an excellent summer.

The defector sat on the bench in the garden of his house in Bossington Lane admiring the view across Porlock Bay. His flat in a dreary Moscow suburb was now a distant memory.

There was fevered gossip in the village. Exmoor was in the head-lines, not just in the British press but worldwide. For a trial at Exeter following the shooting of a Great Dane just off the A39, journalists had packed the Crown Court, hoping to hear further details of a bizarre plot to kill the dog-walker that might have involved Jeremy Thorpe, the Liberal Party leader and North Devon MP.

Thorpe wasn't the only topic of conversation. The unexpected news about Harold Wilson had left the Labour Party in turmoil and the country in limbo. Publicly, Wilson had not provided any reason for his quitting No. 10, although he had confided to close colleagues and friends that he worried about succumbing to Alzheimer's Disease, as his father had done; he certainly feared that he might become incapacitated while still holding office.

The truth, however, lay in a visit, days earlier, of one of the heads of Britain's intelligence services, who had in silence showed the Prime Minister the damming written statement of a KGB officer which

---

* This story was written many months before the KGB defector Alexander Litvinenko was poisoned by polonium in London.

finally confirmed long held but previously unsubstantiated suspicions. On offer was a forced retirement, with pension. The alternative was disclosure and public disgrace.

Once a week, the defector strolled down to the Ship Inn for a beer
or two. His MI5 controllers had long advised him to assimilate into
the local community. Often he played dominoes and engaged other
drinkers in conversation, assiduously avoiding political issues. In the
bar there had often been questions about his accent and his ante-
cedents. The defector's response was consistent. He had fled Czechoslovakia when the Russian tanks had entered its capital to quell the
uprising in the Prague Spring of 1968 and had been granted political asylum. No one questioned that plausible explanation.

✶

The defector had been the chief KGB assassin in the sinister Department 13, known within the Lubyanka as the 'Department of Wet
Tricks'. But he had grown tired of his art. His last 'kill' had been
difficult. Using the cover of an immigration officer in the Russian
Embassy in London, he had sprayed a highly toxic substance onto
the travel documents collected in person by a high-ranking British
politician.

A month later, while staying at the KGB headquarters in Karlhorst,
in East Berlin, he had made up his mind to defect. It was a heart-
wrenching decision, made in a quiet bar off the Unter den Linden
where he had gone to drown his sorrows. He was fully aware that the
KGB had a standard procedure for dealing with defectors. They were
chased, wherever they were, and liquidated when they were found. If
a defector took his family with him, they too were at risk. Reluctantly
he took the decision to leave his family in Russia. There would still
be the inevitable retribution, probably banishment to a community
far from Moscow for life. Their lives would be spared but their
privileged existence would be at an end.

Using a telephone in the bar he had called home. It was the last
time he would ever do so. His wife Irena, sensing something was
wrong, was soon in tears. He had spoken softly to his daughter

Valentina, one of the brightest students at the prestigious School No. 6, an establishment reserved for the children of senior KGB officers. Even a hardened killer, one of the best the KGB had ever produced, could cry; tears had welled up as he spoke to them both. Forever they would bear the scars of being the wife and daughter of a defector. School No. 6 for Valentina would be replaced by a school which at best turned out panel-beaters for the new factories of Kuibyshev or the appalling mining towns around Lake Baikal, far to the east. Any thought of becoming a doctor would now have to be abandoned.

In West Berlin the British had, within hours, spirited him away to RAF Gatow. By evening the military transport was touching down at the highly secure RAF Boscombe Down, the operational bomber airfield in Wiltshire. London was not the destination for the series of interrogations; neither was any of the usual 'safe houses' in other parts of the country – they might be compromised by the Soviets.

The news that the most prolific killer in the KGB's 'Department of Wet Tricks' had defected reached only a select few. Members of the Cabinet were deliberately kept out of the loop, even the Prime Minister, such was the intense secrecy needed to protect the man who had offered to disclose every political assassination of the Cold War undertaken by the KGB and the GRU, the intelligence arm of the Red Army. His KGB codename was 'Gromov', the signature that British Intelligence was aware had been responsible for several killings in Britain, including that of a respected trades union official who had discovered that his union leader had been on the Moscow payroll for many years. There was the promise of MI5 protection from KGB assassination teams, but the defector knew that one day they would find him. They were good. He had trained them in their art.

For three weeks he had been ensconced in a guest house on the south coast, the 'owners', a highly trusted husband and wife team having been brought out of retirement for this operation. They were long forgotten by present operatives of both MI5 and MI6. He was the only guest. Cruising the streets outside were four newly 'retired'

officers from Special Branch, diligent veterans of the conflict in Northern Ireland and completely reliable.

The defector's job had been to kill, to follow orders not just from General Nikolay Rodin, the head of his department, but also directly from the Central Committee. Always he operated in the shadows, but his name was feared within the Organisation. Only a few could claim to know him.

He provided, to the joint MI5 and MI6 interrogators, names – but names only of those who were dead, his victims. He omitted the name of his final and most celebrated victim, whose death accomplished a long-standing Russian plan to kill a leading international politician and install someone 'friendly' towards the USSR.

During one of the interrogations, recorded on tape in an adjoining room by two alert MI5 scientific branch officers, an interrogator had written down a question on a piece of paper and given it to the defector. The defector got up and walked around the room. He asked

for some water. The 'listeners' next door were unaware of what was happening.

For a while the defector considered a response, but eventually he sat down, returned the piece of paper and remained silent. Over the next month, the interrogators probed again many times, but the response was the same. Eventually the interrogations ceased.

*

'Comrade, admiring the view?' asked the voice softly.

The defector turned slowly around to face his uninvited visitor.

'Comrade, not even the British could hide you away for ever.'

The defector recognised in those blue steely eyes the same intense glare that he had fixed on his own victims. They were the eyes of an assassin.

'We have loose ends, Comrade – standard Department 13 procedure.'

'Any point in asking how you found me?'

The visitor smiled broadly.

'We found you years ago. We took photographs and sent them back to Moscow so the Centre could confirm that it was you. On several occasions we tailed you around Porlock. We even sat behind you in the village church. What were you doing there? Asking for redemption?'

'So why did you wait?'

'Good question, Comrade. Department 13 wanted you dead, the fate of all traitors, but someone on the Central Committee ordered us to leave you alone. You must have had powerful friends. A week ago our group received new orders. Our people in Britain reported that Mr Wilson was on the brink of resigning. Your life had to be terminated. It was the end of an illegal operation by the department, one not approved by the Central Committee.'

The defector gently slid his hand into a trouser pocket where he always kept his small-calibre firearm, but the movement was not lost on the visitor.

'So, Comrade, what did you tell them?'

'As little as I felt I could get away with, to try to limit the punishment of my wife and daughter. In Berlin I had promised more. Once in England I didn't keep to that promise. They were annoyed.'

'Surely MI5 was more persuasive, Comrade? Didn't they suggest a flight with them in a helicopter over the North Sea – that well-used British method? They suspend their victims head-first over the side, letting one leg go and holding on to the other, but slowing losing their grip. That treatment makes most of them talk. But several of our past Comrades have been killed that way.'

'I gave them only the names of everyone I had assassinated, all thirty. Dead, their names are of limited use.'

'Comrade, your memory must be muddled by your decadent lifestyle. Your file says thirty-one.'

For a second the quiet was punctured by noise from Bossington Beach. Both men looked in the direction of a large group of young boys, shouting excitedly as they ran along the stones.

It was an opportunity. The defector pulled out his gun but the visitor, a much younger man, knocked it out of his hand. They struggled, but it was unequal.

The defector suddenly felt a sharp and stinging pain in his neck. He collapsed to the ground on his knees. The assassin, now smiling, rolled up a sleeve of his suit. Strapped to his forearm was a cylindrical apparatus that resembled a cigar holder, but was smaller. A wire protruded, connected to the small button of a firing mechanism that was discreetly taped into the palm of his hand.

'How many men have *you* killed,' the defector said weakly, resigned to his ultimate fate.

'Enough, Comrade, but I think your record may well stand the test of time.'

'What is the poison? I have a right to know before my death.'

'Butterflies, Comrade, the same drug you used on your thirty-first victim.'

'Butterflies …?'

'Comrade, your memory. It will come to you.'

'Please, please do something for me?'

The assassin bent down and listened to the defector's request before disappearing as silently as he had arrived.

The defector got up and sat slumped on the bench, staring resignedly at the boys throwing stones into the sea. He knew that within twenty-four hours the injected toxin would begin its attack on his vital organs.

He had been given 'The Devil's Bullet', one of the chosen methods of KGB assassination and the most difficult for any foreign intelligence service to verify.

The injected substance was a two-part concoction. The first element was a masking drug that would almost immediately induce a massive dose of influenza which would cover the induction of the second, which would be lethal. The 'Devil's Bullet' would ensure that by the end of the week he would be dead. There was no cure.

★

The defector *had* in fact informed his interrogators about his thirty-first operation.

After the interrogations had ceased, MI5 had moved him to Porlock, an area considered safe from the KGB. Panic buttons had been installed around the house, linked directly to a regional MI5 office in the West Country. He was expected to phone in every evening at a specific time. Some days he had forgotten to and was admonished.

One day in December 1975 he had been advised that two MI5 officers from London wanted to discuss some matters with him. One was a woman, young and attractive, who spoke fluent Russian. She surprised him by saying that she had news of his family. The defector was ecstatic.

The woman returned several times over the next few weeks, on her own and with the promise that a message could be delivered to his family. There was a price, but this time he didn't hold back.

*

The plot to murder a British politician was a KGB operation that Vladimir Yefimovich Semichastny, the head of the KGB, had shared with only three members of the Soviet intelligence organisation. Many officers, including his six deputies, were too close to the Central Committee, the Praesidium, and to Nikita Khrushchev. Under Khrushchev the KGB had been 'modernised' and to Semichastny's great dismay it had lost much of its autonomy. It was now mandatory for permission to be sought of the Central Committee for the most sensitive of KGB missions. For what Semichastny was planning, no authority would be sought.

Nothing exists on paper concerning the meeting in November 1962 at a KGB safe house in the Serevrjannombor, the Silver Forest, ten miles outside Moscow. The venue for the meeting had been well chosen, away from the prying eyes of Kremlin stooges and the British, who systematically deployed directional electronic listening bugs throughout Moscow. These were small enough to be embedded in the branches of trees in parks facing Soviet government buildings and facilities. To the KGB the British were the most devious of intelligence enemies.

Semichastny's chauffeur tentatively steered a path along the recently cleared driveway in the forest, where the oaks and pines bent under the weight of the heavy snowfalls.

Semichastny was the first to arrive. He strolled into the study of the dacha and poured himself a stiff drink. The trusted housekeeper always kept a good supply of Scottish malt for the Chairman. In front of the roaring log fire, relishing its warmth, the head of the KGB perused the paintings around the walls. In Stalin's day official photographs of the dictator had been the norm. Now they were gone. Just like Stalin, his body rotting in his coffin in the Kremlin wall.

Khrushchev had begun the process of democratisation in an attempt to release the economy from the dead hand of the Communist state. Too much bureaucracy was to the detriment of the economy, a constraint on his bid to make Russia the economic equivalent of America. Central planning was necessary, but not at any price. His radical policies had detractors, Semichastny being one. To the Chairman of the KGB, the duplication of Western economic practices spelt failure – and weakness in the eyes of the people. Even worse was Khrushchev's rapprochement to the West on foreign affairs. Russia was a superpower but it didn't flex enough its military muscle. There were endless whispers in the Kremlin about a possible coup. One was true. Semichastny, with Leonid Brezhnev and Nikolay Podgorny, was plotting Khrushchev's downfall. Key areas within the Kremlin had been bugged, even Khrushchev's private quarters. Evidence was being gathered to be used to portray Khrushchev as a traitor to the State.

Second to arrive at the dacha in the Silver Forest was Colonel Alexander Suntsov, a KGB officer in his forties, a careerist who had been selected for training at the KGB school after university. Smart, ambitious and good-looking, Suntsov was a popular choice to run the desk in the Lubyanka that managed agents in Britain, Australia, Malta, Cyprus and Scandinavia. His was one of the most prestigious

appointments within the organisation. Suntsov was an officer
Semichastny felt he could trust implicitly.

Outside the dacha all was quiet. The two drivers huddled in one
car for warmth, turning the engine over from time to time.

The third person to arrive was Basil Vasiliyevich Naumov, a man
in his late fifties. He slowly opened his briefcase and extracted two
sheets of paper. He had typed them up himself that day in the
privacy of his home near the centre of Moscow. When he had

accomplished his task, Naumov had extracted the ribbon from the typewriter and burned it in an ashtray. In his long career in the KGB he had learned to protect his back – he would live longer that way.

As a pharmacologist, Naumov's brief wasn't to dispense or invent drugs to cure the sick; he was an executioner in a white coat. In the Lubyanka his regular appearance roused tension and fear. Employees hurried past Naumov in the corridors, avoiding eye contact and never offering any salutation. He had served as deputy to the notorious Professor Grigori Maironovsky, the poisoner of the Swedish diplomat Raul Wallenberg in his Lubyanka cell and executioner of countless political opponents of both Stalin and Beria. Maironovsky and Naumov had perfected their art. They could administer poison in such a way that it would remain undetected. The cause of death of their victims would be put down to natural causes such as heart failure.

Naumov handed the papers to Semichastny and Suntsov, then sat back to allow them to study what was, in his opinion, one of the most ingenious achievements of Toxicological Laboratory No. 12, the infamous 'Laboratory X', one of three such KGB laboratories.

Semichastny and Suntsov knew that there was only one man for this operation. Suntsov was instructed to make the arrangements.

*

It was at 9.12 pm on January 18, 1963 that Dr Walter Somerville, consultant cardiologist to the Middlesex Hospital, announced that '*Mr Gaitskell's heart condition deteriorated suddenly and he died peacefully.*' Hugh Gaitskell was 56. The pressmen were having their own briefing in another room in the hospital. '*The death was sudden and peaceful,*' stated Percy Clark, the Labour Party spokesman. '*He had shown great courage and had put up a tremendous fight for his life.*'

In the course of the following days messages of sympathy were received from world leaders. Khrushchev, in his message of condolence, said that he was '*particularly grieved*' and referred to Gaitskell as an outstanding political leader who would have been a welcome guest in Moscow on his forthcoming trip. Harold Wilson, now one of the main contenders in the forthcoming fight to head the party, described Gaitskell's death as a '*tragic loss*', especially as Labour, in his opinion, was poised for election victory.

Gaitskell was cremated on January 23, but not before an autopsy had proved inconclusive. It did not explain how a flu virus had resulted in the almost complete breakdown of his organs. MI5, even before Gaitskell's death, had taken a major interest in the illness that had so quickly befallen the Labour leader. On his death, they arranged for organ tissue to be sent to Porton Down, the highly secret government laboratory in Wiltshire which led the world in the development of chemical and germ warfare, for analysis. Peter Wright, an MI5 officer who specialised in scientific and techno-logical matters, received the results.

The Porton Down scientists confirmed a severe case of the sys-temic variant *lupus erythematosus,* a disease extremely rare in Britain, and then usually seen in women. They could not conclude how Gaitskell had contacted it. Enquiries were discreetly made by MI5 and MI6 in Moscow, and in other Eastern European capitals, on whether Gaitskell had been the victim of the infamous 'Laboratory X'. No agent could confirm that suspicion.

In Moscow *Pravda* reported the death and announced that the British Labour Party would select a new leader on February 14. There were several candidates, including Harold Wilson, the Shadow Foreign Secretary. Someone the Russian Intelligence Services had groomed since his first visit to Moscow during World War Two might now be about to achieve the very highest political office.

✶

In the Ship Inn the regulars enquired of the barman whether their Czech friend had been in lately. The barman shook his head.

The body never had a burial. Immediately after the assassin had left, the defector had pushed a panic alarm and a private ambulance was rushed to Porlock. Within hours the house was 'cleaned'. The doctors at Porton Down tried to save the defector, but they knew they werc powerless. Red scaly marks first appeared on his nose, then spread quickly to his scalp, lips and cheeks. These marks then turned a brighter red and took on the shape of butterflies. Soon they appeared all over his body. Within a day the lupus virus had affected his lungs and heart. By the seventh day kidney function had ceased, and all the other major organs were failing. Death came as a relief.

In London an urgent meeting was convened to discuss how to dispose of the body. There couldn't be a burial as a death certificate would then be required. Given the strange circumstances of the defector's death, the coroner would ask for an autopsy.

A helicopter was summoned and the body was made ready. In the air the cadaver was chained to a large slab of concrete and tipped out into the murky depths of the North Sea.

★

In Kuibyshev a plain-clothes KGB officer knocked on the door of a run-down apartment. The door was answered by an attractive young woman with bright eyes. She was a doctor, much respected in the community, who had spent her evenings studying after working in the factory. The officer said nothing, but offered her what was in his hand. It had been taken from the defector's study in Porlock – a faded photograph of a father standing proudly with his arms around his young daughter.

On the reverse, in English, were words the defector had written in great despair: 'Valentina … please forgive me.'

### Fact

The term 'The Devil's Bullet' has existed in Russian Intelligence circles for many years. There is a 'Department of Wet Tricks' in Russian Intelligence which has carried out political assassinations and murders in many countries. Any defecting officer of the Russian Intelligence Services is for the rest of his life under a Moscow sentence of death, whatever the cause of the defection. Alexander Litvinenko was an FSB defector and was always at risk of execution in London especially as his location was known. Other KGB defectors, such as Oleg Gordievsky and Oleg Kalugin, who respectively reside in Britain and America go to great lengths to conceal their whereabouts even though they are regular contributors on radio and television on Russian matters. The British authorities were able to pinpoint precisely the Russian assassin, and his trail via the Moscow Embassy, British Airways flights from and to Moscow, and London hotels and restaurants as they had a hand-held device that could detect the barest trace of polonium. This came as a major surprise to the Russians who mistakenly believed that the British didn't possess such a portable instrument.

Moscow religiously maintains a list of all defectors from the Russian Intelligence Services and dossiers are maintained on any sightings. Most defectors go to ground in whichever country they defect to, keen that their identities are forever hidden. For those defectors who prefer not to maintain this chosen route, the threat of assassination remains very real.

Alexander Litvinenko worked from time-to-time for a research company in London that was a subsidiary of one of the many London-based private security companies that have mushroomed since the invasion of Iraq and the actions in Afghanistan, providing information on Russian companies and key people who now possess much of Russia's vast wealth.

This Russian defector who was experienced in the battleground of Chechnya knew full well the risks he took by operating as he did in London. He paid the price with his life – by the action of an assassin who gave him 'The Devil's Bullet'.

# Sin and Redemption

## SATURDAY, SEPTEMBER 7, 1940 – DAY 371 OF THE WAR

T HE WEATHER FORECAST for the South West was fair, with some light haze. It had been a good summer after a horrible winter when heavy snowfalls had closed many roads over Exmoor for weeks. No snow ploughs had been available, given the shortage of petrol. Farmers with their tractors had helped where they could.

Exmoor was in the grip of war. The Battle of Britain raged over the Bristol Channel and South Wales.

At RAF stations throughout Britain checks were made on what fighter aircraft would be available for combat that day. There was an expectation that this weekend would make or break the RAF in the face of an overwhelming German aerial onslaught. The RAF reported to the War Cabinet at 9 am that it had 398 serviceable Hurricanes, 223 Spitfires, 44 Blenheims, 20 Defiant night fighters and 9 Gloster Gladiators to defend the country – a total strength of 694 aircraft, compared to 740 two weeks earlier.

*

The sound of ringing church bells the length and breadth of Britain were to be the harbinger that *it* had begun. Across the English Channel, aerial photographs taken by the RAF had confirmed that hundreds of barges had been towed into their final positions in the strategic ports of northern France for the invading army to occupy. There was a general resignation throughout the country that invasion was both imminent and inevitable. Since the evacuation of the British army at Dunkirk in June the whole country had collectively held its breath, fearing the worst. This was not a time to fall ill in Britain. Hospitals had been closed in recent weeks to general admissions, and operations restricted to emergencies. Wards had been cleared for the huge number of casualties expected in the invasion.

German propaganda since the defeat of the British Expeditionary Force and the Dunkirk evacuation had persistently stressed that invasion would become a reality if Britain did not come to heel. In a rousing speech at the Reichstag in Berlin on July 19, three days after British bombs had hit the southern German city of Freiburg, killing 57 inhabitants including 22 children in their classroom, an irate Hitler had made a final public attempt to persuade Britain to negotiate a peace settlement. There were no concrete proposals; it was propaganda rather than a serious offer.

'*A great empire will be destroyed,*' ranted Hitler, '*a world empire that I never intended to destroy or even damage. But it is clear to me that the continuation of this struggle will end with the complete destruction of one of the two opponents. Mr Churchill may believe that this will be Germany. I know it will be England.*

'*I regret the sacrifices it will demand. I would like to spare my own people them also. I know that millions of German men and youths are aglow with the thought of at last being able to face the enemy who has declared war on us for the second time and for no reason.*

'*Mr Churchill may reject this declaration of mine by shouting that it is only the product of my fear and my doubts of final victory. But at least I have relieved my conscience before the events that threaten ...*'

Hitler avoided telling his people that the bombs that had killed many in Freiburg in an earlier raid on May 10 had been manufactured in Germany, not England. The Luftwaffe had dropped the bombs in error during a flying exercise over the city that had gone terrifyingly wrong. The Nazi propaganda machine wasted no time in spinning the line that British airmen had massacred children in schools and patients in the city's hospitals.

Despite the public rhetoric, in private, in conversations with his small coterie of trusted generals, Hitler prevaricated at length over whether an invasion could succeed militarily, or indeed whether it was necessary at all if America continued its policy of keeping out of the war. The real enemy, Hitler believed, was not England, it was Russia – a long-held view which Hitler had expressed in his bestselling book, *Mein Kampf*. If he could somehow convince Britain to forge a peace, a military alliance could see off Bolshevism for good. On August 2 the Luftwaffe had dropped tens of thousands of leaflets over Southern England, warning of the dire consequences if Mr Churchill continued to resist. Bundles of these leaflets were also dropped over Swansea and collected by excited schoolchildren.

There were several prongs to the planned German invasion. Troops, with Luftwaffe cover, would land along the coast between Ramsgate and Brighton, and paratroopers would be dropped several miles inland. More landing craft would come ashore between Lyme Regis and Portsmouth. Given the immense importance of the Bristol Channel, a third prong to the German invasion was also anticipated by the British War Office. The capture of Bristol would give the Germans a major bridgehead in the west.

Porlock and its environs fell within the General Headquarters, GHQ, line of defence that extended from Burnham-on-Sea, on the west coast of Somerset, eastwards to Kent. There were key tactical stoplines where the enemy would have to be held in any way possible. Anti-invasion construction had begun in earnest after Dunkirk but the War Cabinet conceded that there was little time left to mount an island defence.

Of significant importance was Taunton, on the stopline that ran from the mouth of the River Parrett on the north Somerset coast down to the mouth of the River Axe on the Devon coast. This stopline was heavily defended with pillboxes, gun emplacements and anti-tank obstacles. Some twenty-one pillboxes were built in the strategic areas of Somerset, some of them disguised. At Lyng a pillbox resembled a haystack, at Old Cleeve one looked like a small

building and at Bossington and Porlock Weir pillboxes were faced
with stones and shingle to merge into the beach. In Minehead naval
engineers dismantled the pier and replaced it with a big naval
gun, capable of dispensing shells that could take out even the
largest German invasion craft. On news of an invasion, bridges
would be blown up and railway tracks demolished by British sappers.
On the roads that passed through Exmoor red flags warned the public not to encroach as artillery regiments were practising. Most road
signs had been taken down. Beaches, such as Bossington, were
off-limits.

  All towns and large villages throughout the country had formed
their own units of Local Defence Volunteers who trained with barely
a usable weapon between them. Even useless ancient rifles from
Britain's theatres were used for parading. By July 8 the ranks of the
volunteers had mushroomed to 1,060,000, but the War Office feared

that this dedicated Home Guard would be powerless against a battle-hardened SS and Wehrmacht.

*

The Bristol Channel was of undoubted strategic importance. Its ports were vital to Britain: important supplies and raw materials flowed in from its global empire and other friendly trading partners, including America. South Wales was also vital to the war effort, and not just for its coal. There were many industrial and key munitions-producing centres. This importance was well understood by the Germans, who had amassed a large archive of aerial photographs taken during the late 1930s. Ack-ack guns now defended the ports. In Swansea, the 64th LAA battery set up Lewis guns in its marine fortification. Bofors and twin-Vickers guns were also erected and during night raids tracer bullets would light up the sky. On Swansea beach large amounts of timber and tree trunks were embedded to discourage enemy glider landings. Fire watchers sat atop buildings, armed only with buckets of sand. Minesweepers daily swept the Channel for mines dropped by the Luftwaffe in their raids. Oil tankers carrying vital aviation fuel were prime targets for the mines, as were the destroyers and other warships that used the ports for refuelling before venturing out into the Atlantic. Schoolchildren in Porlock would count the number of ships in the convoys. Sighting up to twenty-one ships was common.

Searchlight batteries had been constructed on both sides of the Bristol Channel in positions with the widest possible outlook and trees were felled where necessary to enhance the line of sight. One searchlight battery was near the top of the Toll Road between Porlock Weir and Culbone, in a field clear of obstructions. From its commanding position the coast of South Wales was clearly visible, as was the long expanse of Bossington.

The Toll Road battery consisted of two powerful searchlights powered by generators. Anyone who ventured too close was forcibly turned away by a sergeant, a stickler for preserving the secrecy of the unit he commanded. Even inquisitive local children, who took up the challenge to determine what was in the three recently-constructed brick buildings and under the canvas, were chased away. The twin beams criss-crossing the sky were a regular sight. Their operators were billeted in either Porlock or Lynton, but given their arduous nightly routine they often just collapsed into bunks in the huts on site when given permission to stand down.

✶

Concealment of the searchlight battery was difficult, but at the secret establishment on the wild Brendon Common, close to the road that runs south from Brendon to Simonsbath, curious inhabitants of Exmoor ran the risk of being shot on sight if they ventured too close. A small unit of the Royal Engineers, 982 Chemical Warfare Company, were its inhabitants – a hastily formed group of men who had, prior to this posting, undergone a week's basic training at Porton Down,

Britain's experimentation centre for chemical warfare. On the day they arrived in Porlock they were ordered out of their trucks and told to march up Porlock Hill in full battledress, to toughen up. The trucks took the men on to Brendon Manor, where they were to be billeted. This wasn't far from the newly constructed fenced-off compound on Brendon Common.

Jack Edwards, a local man who was also a resident of Brendon Manor, had been handed two important responsibilities by the military. First, he was told to clear the moor area between Brendon Common and Larkborough of all grazing and wild animals. The second instruction was to empty Larkborough farmhouse of all its contents. This he did, selling as much as he could to anyone who made an offer. The signs were then erected that banned all residents and visitors from the moor. The whole site was now out of bounds.

In the following days the farmhouse was used in target practice and smashed to pieces. Within the compound on Brendon Common a large store of artillery shells was housed, as well as a secret consignment for the use of 982 Chemical Warfare Company.

An RAF convoy of lorries had driven slowly through Porlock with a deadly manifest of several hundred 25-pound bombs in packing cases. These were no ordinary bombs to be dropped out of the bomb bays of aircraft. They had been adapted, their warheads filled with mustard gas. In the rear, holes had been drilled to position sticks of cordite, with fuses. On Brendon Common these bombs-turned-rockets were placed in lines in large portable metal troughs, six feet in length, which were suspended on adjustable legs. Nicknamed 'crickets' by the men who operated them, because of their shape, these troughs were set up in series. Once adjusted, rockets could be fired at different angles. The firing mechanism was crude: a tug on a length of string attached to the lead rocket would in turn ignite the rockets in each trough. Up to 192 could be fired at any one time, and they would have a range of four miles. The men of 982 practised vigorously until they could launch their deadly weapons in fifteen minutes.

Given the highly toxic nature of their work and the likely chance of accidents, at Porton Down the unit had been instructed in safety procedures. Simulating a spill, they had rubbed liquid mustard gas onto the backs of their hands, then quickly applied a special cream to prevent blistering. The mustard gas on Brendon Common was stored in 40-gallon oil drums, and well guarded.

During the weekend of September 7-8, 1940, the men on Brendon Common were on full alert, ready to transport their crickets to wherever they were ordered to go. All the crickets had been prepared. If the Germans landed within range, a barrage of mustard gas the like of which had not been experienced since World War One would be sucked into the air on impact. No consideration had been given to the inhabitants of Exmoor, or to anyone who lived close to similar sites elsewhere in southern England where such weapons were primed. Britain was at war and the barbarians were at the gate. Its very survival was under threat. Drastic measures were needed – whatever the human cost.

## THE SKIES OVER BRITAIN WERE QUIET AT 6AM ON SEPTEMBER 7

The men of the searchlight battery on the Porlock to Culbone Toll Road were resting in the huts after an exhausting night. There had been three air raid warnings in Bridgend, the last at 11.51 pm. Barry and Maesteg had been bombed but Swansea had been spared. RAF Twynells had called in the early morning with the news that the last of the German bombers had peeled away over the Bristol Channel, heading south to their bases in France.

Taff and Oded were too exhausted to sleep. The sergeant had taken the unit's army motorbike and hadn't returned yet.

'Are *you* scared?' enquired Taff of his colleague who was immersed in a novel in his bunk.

'Maybe, Taff, maybe,' came the muffled and uninterested response.

'Will *it* happen today?' Taff solicited, staring out of the window at the Bristol Channel and the dawn of a new day, disappointed by the slow reaction.

'You mean the invasion?' grunted Oded, annoyed at another interruption.

'Of course I do,' responded Taff.

Oded raised his eyes and saw the young Welshman's concern. Reluctantly he turned down the corner of the page and sat up. Before he could respond the door of the hut was thrown open and the sergeant, a bull of a man, stormed in and flopped into a chair, smelling of drink.

'What are you two on about *now?*' snarled the unit's NCO. He pointed to the kettle, expecting Taff to boil up a brew.

'Taff asked whether I'd be scared if the Germans came,' replied Oded cautiously. Previous experience had warned him that it was unwise to engage the volatile sergeant in too stimulating a conversation after he had been drinking. It was usual for the landlord of the pub in Contisbury, The Blue Ball, to leave the back door open all hours so his army regulars could help themselves to a drink and leave their money on the bar. In the early hours of the morning it wasn't unusual to see army motor vehicles parked outside.

'What did you say, son? What rich pearls of wisdom did an intelligent Jew like yourself impart to our young man from Swansea?'

'Nothing, sergeant, *nothing,*' retorted Oded, sullenly picking up his book.

'Typical,' sneered the sergeant. 'You never get a straight answer out of a *Jew.*'

Oded jumped off the bunk, his fists clenched ready for a confrontation with the NCO, who had taken great delight in riling him since his recent posting to the searchlight battery.

'No, Oded!' shouted Taff. 'Leave it … please, *please!*'

There was a smirk on the sergeant's face as Taff shoved Oded away.

Oded returned to his bunk, angry with Taff for stepping in. How he detested the sergeant. Since his posting to the Toll Road the sergeant had constantly taunted him, openly boasting that he had once been a Mosley Blackshirt, a Jew-baiter.

The advice from his father had for years rung in his ears. 'Don't get angry, walk away,' was the instruction his father had given him when, as a boy growing up in Göttingen in Germany, he had been pilloried and ostracised at school because of his faith. After Hitler was elected Chancellor in January 1933, the Jews in Germany feared the worst. In Göttingen, as elsewhere, they were banned from the town's swimming baths and other public buildings and treated as lepers in German society – an *untermenschen*. At school Oded had been called names, unrepeatable names, and taunted as he walked home. His father, a physicist, had taught physics at the world-famous Göttingen University but the SS had ordered the university authorities to withdraw his *venia legendi*, the certificate needed to teach in the university system. Imperial Chemical Industries, Britain's largest industrial company, offered him a position in Oxford, to work and teach, worth £300 a year. He accepted it, and other Jewish scientists did likewise.

Immensely relieved, the family had packed their bags and caught a train to Holland and a boat to England. Two years after they arrived in Oxford they faced the awful possibility that they might have to return to the clutches of the SS. The ICI bursary expired and was not renewed, and there were no other job offers in England. Oded's father had reluctantly considered work in Venezuela or South Africa, but declined. Oded heard his parents quietly discussing a well-paid offer to work at the premier physics institute in Leningrad but the Russian offer was eventually refused.

New challenges arose for the Jewish scientific community that had settled in the Oxford suburb of Summertown. As the threat of war with Germany grew, so did local suspicion that a fifth-column had been established in its midst. Oded's family home was often visited by the police, called out by neighbours suspicious of anyone who passed through the front door. The German community quickly resolved to speak only English in public.

When war with Germany broke out Oded's father was rounded up by the police with other German immigrants and interned in a camp for aliens on the Isle of Man, others were shipped to a similar camp in Canada. But intervention by the renowned Clarendon Laboratory in Oxford, which was eager to make use of his skills in experimental physics, and the laboratory's government paymasters, enabled Oded's father to become a naturalised British citizen for secret government research.

Oded, now legally British, enlisted in the army, eager to avenge the torment his family had endured in Germany. He had hoped to fight in France and was bitterly disappointed when his regiment remained in Britain on defence duties. Manning a number of searchlight batteries had been Oded's contribution to the war effort to date. He made the best of it.

In the hut, the threatening mood did not recede. Taff offered to make more tea. The sergeant continued to read his paper. Oded, pretending to concentrate on his book, now felt relieved that Taff had intervened as he did. Hitting an NCO was usually punished by a jail sentence, and hard labour.

'Ever met a Jerry?' the sergeant asked Taff as he accepted his tea.

'No, sergeant, where would I have met one?'

'I *have* … several times,' said the sergeant very slowly, milking the effect this statement had on his two juniors.

'Where?' queried Oded, intrigued.

'In pubs … in East London where the British Union of Fascists had its powerbase. The SS first visited our organisation in 1935 under the guise of German tourists eager to sample London's huge variety of culture. They arrived in England in their civvies but with their SS uniforms in their luggage. Once in the pub, we would lock the doors and they would put on their kit and goose-step around. We joined them in our black shirts, black ties, leather belts and boots. In the group photographs we all clicked our heels, stood to attention and gave the Nazi salute. Literature was swapped. We presented them with signed copies of *The Fascist*, our magazine, and they gave us presentation copies of *Mein Kampf* with the NSDAP logo stamped on the cover, and the signature of Baldur von Shirach, the head of the Hitler Youth movement. I even corresponded with one of them for a while, a corporal from Hamburg.'

'I suppose goose-stepping around with SS thugs made you feel *really* superior, sergeant. You're nothing better than a collaborator!' jibed Oded contemptuously.

The chair was thrown to the ground as the sergeant leapt on Oded, dragging him from the bunk to pin him hard against the wall, a large hand tightening around his neck.

Taff was terrified, rooted to the spot.

'Don't lecture *me*, son. See these stripes?' the sergeant snarled into Oded's face.

'That doesn't give you the right to make our lives a bloody misery. You're a bully and a bloody bigot. Heaven help us if *you* ever get to the Front,' Oded gasped. The hand increased its pressure like a vice on his windpipe.

Despite his slender frame, Taff jumped on the back of the sergeant in an attempt to pull him off. His efforts were enough, and Oded slumped to the floor, retching.

'I'm a good soldier!' yelled the sergeant at Oded. 'I fight for my King and country, you hear? One day I'll get into the *real* fighting, not hanging around a hut with a bloody Welsh grammar school boy who mopes about quoting an obscure Welsh poet called Dylan Thomas and a smug Jewish know-it-all. If you *really* want to know, I'm bloody ashamed of what I did as a Blackshirt. Does that make you feel better? Yes, I beat up Jews. And not just Jews – I also gave Communists a right kicking. I didn't come from a family like yours, privileged. Didn't you say your father was a scientist in Germany? What's he doing now for *our* war effort? Nothing, I bet … just whinging with all the other pitiful Jews who came here in the 1930s.'

'Why do you hate Jews so?' wheezed Oded, still trying to recover his breath. 'There must be a reason?'

'One day, *son*, I'll tell you.' With that, the sergeant stormed out of the hut, slamming the door behind him.

'Phew, Oded! You were either bloody brave or just bloody stupid!' whistled Taff, relieved.

'That man has a secret, Taff, I know it. I'm going to clean my searchlight and check the fuel for the generator.'

'I'll stay here,' said Taff, 'I need to complete the log for the past 24 hours.'

Outside, Oded sat in the uncomfortable metal seat attached to the searchlight. Operating it was an arduous task, but he would whoop for joy when he caught a German aircraft in its beam, locking on to it so ack-ack batteries could shoot it down. The ack-ack guns would fall silent when the Hurricanes and Spitfires were in the air but the searchlights would continue to sweep the skies. Such effort and concentration left his body continually exhausted. There had been little time for sleep in past weeks since the bombing of South Wales had started in earnest.

Even during daylight the men at the battery had an active role as spotters, reporting any sightings of low-flying German reconnaissance aircraft to two radar establishments on the Pembrokeshire coast. At RAF Warren, operators were able to provide long-range early alerts for the Western approaches and the Bristol Channel. Those at RAF St Twynells provided warnings of low-level approaches to the Bristol Channel with specific cover for Swansea and the industrial complex at Port Talbot.

At dusk the unit would be fully prepared for the long night ahead. Taff would be close to the phone, expecting regular updates from his usual two contacts, Huw at RAF Warren and John at RAF Twynells. The NCO would ensure that the battery was on its toes, barking out orders in his customary way. He was good at that.

After finishing his log Taff joined Oded.

'Any news of your brother, Taff?' asked Oded gently, inhaling the smoke of his cigarette as they lounged against the wall of the hut, gazing towards the Welsh coastline obscured in the early morning haze.

'Nothing. His regiment still hasn't released the names of those who were left behind at Dunkirk.'

'Perhaps he was injured and the Germans have him in a field hospital. Don't give up hope.'

'He's dead, Oded, I sense it. We were very close.'

'How's your family in Swansea? Are they safe?'

'So far, yes. I received a letter yesterday from my mother. Their street hasn't been hit but Dad has become a fire warden. He's usually away all night and Mum worries about him. She says conditions in Swansea are getting worse. Rations have been reduced again and to get something special you have to buy on the black market. There are now very few cars on the streets because of petrol rationing. People are riding bicycles if they can lay their hands on them – many are being nicked. All the street signs have been taken away and at night the street lights stay off so there're many accidents – pedestrians and cyclists get hit by cars with headlights almost totally blacked out. Men in lorries came to our street and took down all the metal garden railings to use as scrap. Mum's concerned about using the Anderson shelter in the garden because several have taken direct hits. Dad's told her that when he's on fire duty she'll be safer in the communal underground shelters in the local church.'

'I hear from my mother in Oxford that rationing is becoming pretty dire but at least Oxford doesn't appear to be a Luftwaffe target,' said Oded.

'The sergeant was pretty rude about your father. What is he working at?'

'When I'm home I do get the gist of what he's doing at the laboratory: it's something to do with uranium, I think. He's in charge of constructing a machine that shakes at a very high speed so that uranium is separated through special membranes.'

'I've never heard of uranium,' responded Taff.

'Nor had I, Taff, until I heard my father mention it. I did ask Dad about it but he put a finger up to his mouth. I think it's a big government secret.'

The early morning mist over the Bristol Channel was beginning to clear. It would be a fine day, and warm. Everything looked calm. The war seemed to be somewhere else, far away.

⋆

From this same observation point on the Toll Road the men of the searchlight battery had from afar helplessly witnessed the first

Luftwaffe attack on Swansea, mid-morning on Thursday, June 27. Thankfully there had been no casualties and, despite the dropping of ten high-explosive bombs, damage had been slight. Later, one lone German bomber circled Swansea before dropping its load over the area of Morriston. Again damage was slight and there were no casualties. The main raid that day was on industrial sites near Bristol. Seven Heinkel aircraft attacked the Filton works of the British Aeroplane Company but the bombs fell into the sea, way off target.

The Luftwaffe had yet to learn that the British had found an ingenious method of intercepting and adjusting the Knickebein, the German navigation and bombing aid. This transmitted a radar beam from positions in German-occupied Europe across to England, which enabled bombers to fly accurately to their targets. Given the increasing number of attacks along the Bristol Channel in June 1940, it was clear to the British that the Knickebein beam was being transmitted over the industrial heartlands of South Wales and to targets in and around Bristol. The extensive dock area of Bristol was attacked on twenty occasions between June and August, and Avonmouth and Cardiff were also raided. During the early months of the attacks British radar scientists successfully 'bent' the Knickebein beams so that the Luftwaffe targeting was imprecise.

Nevertheless, casualties were beginning to mount. One German aircraft flew low over Swansea on July 10 and dropped four bombs on King's Dock, killing twelve dockworkers and wounding twenty-six others. In Devon the inhabitants of Barnstable were repeatedly alarmed as air-raid sirens wailed every time there was an attack on Swansea. What was terrifying was the sight of German raiders circling directly overhead as they waited their turn for the run-in over their Welsh objective. The population of Barnstable had been considerably swollen by large numbers of children evacuated from London. As Swansea was right at the end of the fuel range of many German aircraft it was not unusual to see them turn around and drop their unused payloads over the water.

August saw an intensification of raids over South Wales. Swansea was hit on Saturday, August 10 and thirteen died, including five members of one family in an Anderson shelter. The new aluminium works, the copper works and the docks at Port Talbot were attacked several times, as were Aberavon, Neath and Pontypridd. Local churches were used as landmarks by the Luftwaffe bombers and even they were not spared. Several burned to the ground.

A number of RAF squadrons were charged with the defence of the Bristol Channel, day and night, including the experienced 92 Squadron which had as its motto, 'We Fight or Die'. Robert Stanford Tuck, who had already won the highest honours, was one of its pilots with 'kills' to his name in north-west France, achieved as German fighters harassed the evacuation of Dunkirk. Back in England, the squadron had re-equipped with Spitfires and was sent to RAF Pembrey in South Wales, an airfield south of Kidwelly, near Llanelli. There was one local site there that needed to be defended at all costs. Not far from RAF Pembrey, in the sand dunes of Cefu Sidan, lay the Royal Ordnance factory that employed 2,000 workers and pumped out 700 tons of TNT a year – the largest output in the country.

When 92 Squadron was transferred to RAF Biggin Hill in mid June, defence duties fell to 87 Squadron based at RAF Exeter. They also had considerable experience in France. Over the weekend of September 7-8 another squadron was to join the fray. The Hurricanes of 79 Squadron would land at RAF Pembrey from Biggin Hill. There would be no time for the pilots to train to local conditions. The aircraft were immediately refuelled and made ready, their response now crucial. From August 22 the Luftwaffe replaced the Knickebein with the X-Verfahren, a navigation device that the British scientists would be unable to alter. The Luftwaffe could now bomb with far greater precision, as demonstrated by the raid on the Bristol Aeroplane Company at Filton that day. The RAF now needed to intercept their targets quicker than ever.

The Luftwaffe made another key decision in August. Until then, they had bombed only in daylight, and there had been no Messerschmitt 109 fighter cover as South Wales was beyond their range. This had led to heavy bomber losses. In future, although daylight attacks were not to cease completely, the main thrust was to be their early evening and night flights.

*

Swansea bore the brunt of this new Luftwaffe strategy on September 1.

RAF Warren had urgently called just before 8pm, alerting the searchlight battery on the Toll Road that raiders were expected in the Bristol Channel. The late summer day had been warm and clear. It would not be fully dark until well after 8pm. Until then, the batteries scattered along the coastlines would be powerless to assist.

At 8.15pm RAF Twynells telephoned the battery to report that thirty-one aircraft were approaching the West of England. Bristol docks were the probable target. As the sun was setting the first wave dropped their load of oil bombs on Avonmouth and Portishead in the hope that the wooden structures in the dockyards would be quickly ablaze. By luck they didn't burn, but oil bombs hit surrounding streets and nine people died.

The real devastation that night was reserved for Swansea. The roar of the powerful engines of the aircraft was audible all around the Bristol Channel. Sirens sounded at 8.48pm in Bridgend and minutes later the naval oil depot at Llandarcy was ablaze. Storage tanks erupted in flames, which soared high into the night sky. Firemen could only stand back and let them burn. In the town centre, historic buildings collapsed into the street. The sight of Swansea burning could be seen all along the Devon and West Somerset coast.

Wave after wave of raiders circled, awaiting their run-in to target. That night in the inferno of Swansea 33 died and 115 were injured. Rescue teams clawed with their bare hands to save those trapped, working only by torchlight so as not to attract the attention of aircraft circling in the darkness above. But such precautions were futile as parachute flares hung in trees and on buildings, illuminating Swansea like a giant Christmas tree. The fighters from RAF Pembrey and RAF Exeter tried their best to bring down the raiders. RAF Pembrey was itself hit at 10.40pm.

In the hours ahead there was to be no respite. Barry docks were hit, as was Briton Ferry. A black mantle enveloped Swansea as Llandarcy continued to burn.

✳

Taff came from a family that in the present generation worked in Port Talbot. His father had given up the grime and choking smoke of the power station for gentler employment as a janitor at Swansea Grammar School. Unlike his siblings, Taff had displayed academic talent: he sat the school entrance exam and passed well. There were confident hopes that he might progress to the town's university on a scholarship.

But ambition was put on hold and Taff attempted to enlist – unsuccessfully at first, as he was still too young. To fill his time he worked for a local baker, pulling a heavy cart around the streets. In September 1939 Parliament passed the National Services Act, which made all men between the ages of eighteen and forty-one liable for conscription. Taff handed back the cart and enlisted in the army, asking to join his brother's regiment. This request was denied: Taff, like Oded, was needed for the home defence effort. His army colleagues only infrequently called him by his Christian name, Euan. 'Taff' was the norm, as it was for most Welshmen in the army.

### 7AM ON SEPTEMBER 7

Taff sat waiting by the telephone in the hut, composing a letter home. He had tried to have a nap but he had a nasty feeling about the ugly confrontation between the sergeant and Oded. He feared that worse was to follow.

In other letters home he had omitted any mention of the sergeant, warmly describing instead the camaraderie he shared with his friends. This letter was different. There was an issue he wished to share with his parents. Like Oded, he was a breaking point – not because of the war but as a result of incessant disparagement by his NCO.

Oded had gone for a walk after completing his chores. The sergeant had probably gone to see his girlfriend, a drinking friend from the pub in Contisbury, a married woman whose husband was in the navy, somewhere in the Mediterranean.

After completing his letter, Taff strolled over to the other hut for breakfast. At least on this front the sergeant had a positive use as his girlfriend provided the unit with regular supplies of fresh eggs.

By 9am Oded was back in his bunk reading his book and Taff was aimlessly scanning the newspaper. The sergeant arrived back and Taff made the tea.

'I'm sorry,' said the sergeant sullenly, his usual two-word apology for his outbursts.

'OK, sergeant,' responded Taff, quietly.

Oded smouldered, staying silent, but he was surprised at what Taff posed next.

'Have you read *any* poetry, sergeant?' enquired Taff.

The NCO looked taken aback. 'Don't be daft,' he retorted.

'You said I mope about quoting Dylan Thomas,' Taff continued. He was growing in confidence. 'Mock me if you have to, but don't condemn someone who just might turn out to be one of the greatest poets this country will ever produce. He's a Swansea man, sergeant. Went to the grammar school but before my time. My Dad knew him and *his* Dad who was a teacher at the school. Dylan Thomas was lousy at school but good at writing poetry. He left school at sixteen, same age as me, to work as a reporter on the local paper. He moved to London and then *really* started to write. Ever heard of *Twenty-Five Poems*, sergeant, his first major work?'

There was astonishment on the sergeant's face, and Oded's.

'What's your *point*, lad. Why do I need to hear this drivel?'

'Do not *insult* me just because I like Dylan Thomas. He's *not* obscure as you say – this Welshman's becoming famous, attracting a following all over the country and my Mum says that even in America he has readers.'

Oded was grinning. He wanted to clap his hands. Taff was transformed. No longer the timid lad from Swansea, he was making the sergeant look stupid.

A silence descended upon the hut. Taff and Oded exchanged

glances and confidently stood their ground in unison, in a common resistance to whatever the sergeant might throw at them.

The sergeant, lost for words but with a surly glare, faced the two privates. Taff hadn't finished.

'Sin … and redemption,' said Taff in a slow, measured tone. 'Dylan Thomas talks about sin and redemption in his poetry.'

'Are are you daring to suggest that *I'm* a sinner and I need redemption? I'll knock your block off!' retorted the sergeant, almost choking with anger. Oded moved closer to Taff.

Taff would not go so far as to enunciate the response he had already framed in his letter to his mother. She had bitterly condemned those in Swansea who had gathered in the town centre in 1936 to listen to the ranting diatribes of Sir Oswald Mosley when the leader of the Blackshirts had visited the town.

The ringing telephone pierced the charged atmosphere. The reality of war intruded. It was the first call of the day from Huw at RAF Warren, reporting that no Luftwaffe activity had been detected off any part of the British coastline. But that wasn't the real reason for his call, said Huw. As a fellow Swansea man he had felt the need for a chat with his telephone friend in the searchlight battery. Taff was however a reluctant partner in the conversation, impatient at the interruption.

The moment had passed. Huw soon signed off, detecting that Taff seemed preoccupied. Taff asked the sergeant for permission to leave the battery to stretch his legs. Receiving no response, he took that as a yes. He needed solitude.

*

Curiosity, one very warm morning in July, had led to his discovery of his own quiet place, a place where he could avoid the sergeant for a short time – just long enough to reflect. The dense strange wood near the top of the Toll Road had interested him, enticing him to enter, drawing him into its darkness where the trees were twisted and stunted. At first he had felt afraid, but he walked on until, in the distance, he had seen sunlight. The sun-soaked clearing, covered in inviting lush grass, was mesmerising. Listening to the birdsong he felt compelled to lie down and gaze into the clear blue sky.

That was the first of several visits to the clearing. In these quiet periods of escape from his involvement in the war he would yearn for lost days of innocence when he was a schoolboy playing conkers and 'Who's It?' in the playground. At weekends he and his mates used to cycle to Mumbles and lark around Three Cliffs Bay until the sun went down. To a Swansea schoolboy, Adolf Hitler had been an ogre to be mimicked in the playground with strutting goose-steps and a blackened upper lip. When the teachers saw such daft antics the boys would be admonished.

At the edge of the clearing was a rough-edged upright stone, about two feet high. A circle and, within it, what looked like a multiplication sign had been carved into its flat front suface. When Taff had first seen it he had run his fingers along the grooves, but he was not to touch the stone again. It felt evil. It seemed to be emanating danger.

On his second visit to the clearing Taff had heard rustling in the trees and froze with fear. A young girl emerged, waving. She introduced herself as Margaret Richards. She was one of the six children of the family that lived at Broomstreet Farm, just off the Lynmouth Road. Like her brother and sisters she went to school in Porlock, but often she would hide when the school bus arrived at Broomstreet Gate and play truant for the day. As soon as the bus disappeared she would run off to explore Lilycombe and Culbone woods. She, too, was curious about the stone, and she asked Taff what he made of the symbol. Taff shuddered.

Margaret informed him indignantly that it had been she who had discovered the stone lying face down several years earlier. When she had scraped the moss away and seen the strange markings, she had realised that it was unlike any of the other ancient boundary stones that littered Exmoor. She was surprised, she told Taff, when, in December 1939 and now in January, reports appeared in the local press about a stone of significant historical importance having been discovered near Culbone. A newspaper photographer had taken pictures of what they called 'The Culbone Stone'. An archaeologist suggested that it dated back to the ninth century, but its symbolism baffled him. Margaret insisted to her family and other locals that she had uncovered the stone well before 1939, but no one believed the story of an unreliable young girl with a history of truancy.

Margaret declared to Taff with great satisfaction that she alone knew the whereabouts of at least twenty stones in the area, and she beckoned him deeper into the wood. After scrambling under low branches she pointed to the undisturbed stones, arranged in two rows, poking out of the moss. She made him promise to keep her secret. He nodded in agreement.

Through the remainder of July and August, as the Battle of Britain intensified, Taff found little time to visit his quiet place. When he did there was never any sign of Margaret. But Taff did introduce Oded to the clearing and he too felt touched, even strengthened, by the strange energy that seemed to emanate from it. Here they would smoke and talk, mainly about the sergeant, but about Margaret's hidden stones Taff would keep his silence.

It was in the secret clearing that Taff first confided to Oded how terrified he was of death, particularly of dying alone. Oded tried to reassure him, but to no avail. Taff told him about a poem written by Dylan Thomas entitled 'Death has No Dominion', a curious ode to dead men in a drifting boat whose bones had been picked clean by sea birds and bleached by the strong sun and sea winds. No one knew how they came to be in the boat, or how they had perished; they did not even know their names. Taff felt convinced that every Dylan Thomas poem contained a message, and that in some way the sea would figure in his own death.

Today, after the awful altercation in the hut, when Taff needed his own space and escaped to the clearing to gather his thoughts, it struck him that, although his NCO was undoubtedly a sinner, there was also genuine sadness behind those angry eyes. There was something that had turned the man into what he was.

Taff hadn't been in the clearing long before Oded suddenly emerged from the wood to warn him that the sergeant wanted everyone on the site on parade for inspection. They strolled back to the searchlight battery. The Toll Road was deserted, as it usually was. Oded commented on the colourful light purple flowers of the heather by the roadside.

'You never gave me an answer,' said Taff as he opened the gate to the field, looking ahead to the battery huts.

'To what question?' asked Oded.

'The invasion … Will it be this weekend?'

'No idea, mate, but I'll say one thing. Our blokes will be ready for them. We'll teach the sergeant's SS friends how to fight.'

They walked on in silence. Oded realised that Taff was more on edge than usual. 'Don't worry, mate,' he reassured with a warming smile, 'the sergeant wouldn't really have strangled me. But I certainly touched a nerve.'

'Are *you* scared of death, Oded?'

'Just might be, Taff … just might be.'

## AT 11AM RAF WARREN RANG

Taff hurriedly handed the information to the sergeant. A formation of seventy bombers with a fighter escort was shortly to cross the Kent coast at Folkestone and was expected to split up. Dover and the RAF stations in East Kent were likely targets. Some planes might divert to the Bristol Channel, but that was unlikely. The sergeant put the battery on immediate alert, scanning the skies with binoculars. Any sightings would be reported.

It was a glorious day. The only aircraft the unit saw were Hurricanes practising an attack in a finger-four formation, a system that had begun to rack up 'kills'.

In the early afternoon, after a quick lunch, Oded and Taff sat on the grass outside the hut. The sergeant joined them, offering cigarettes. 'I've brought more eggs,' he said casually. 'We can have a good fry-up in the morning.'

'Thanks, I look forward to that,' said Taff.

Oded nodded his appreciation. Despite his dislike of him, he had to admit that the unit's NCO did run the battery efficiently, and there

were rare occasions when the sergeant did reveal a softer side. When
Taff had one day failed to complete the unit's activity log, a rare lapse,
and the error had been spotted by a visiting officer, the sargeant had
not blamed Taff but had accepted responsibility himself.

The three sat outside the hut smoking, enjoying the sun, chatting
– they looked like colleagues sharing wartime camaraderie. Out in
the Bristol Channel two minesweepers dragged the waters. Oded,
through his binoculars, counted the painted chevrons on their
funnels, which showed the impressive number of mines they had
found and made safe.

The sergeant picked up his newspaper. 'Churchill made a speech
yesterday about the Anglo-American Concord,' he read out. 'The
Yanks are going to give us fifty mothballed destroyers – that should
frighten the Germans,' he mocked. 'Churchill says it's a huge boost
for the war effort. Glory help us.'

The sergeant then laughed out aloud. 'Lads, listen to this. Churchill
has criticised the country's early warning sirens. He calls them "Ban-
shee howlings" – he can't stand the noise and sees no reason why
every siren should go off just because the Luftwaffe is flying overhead
en route to somewhere else.'

'Any news about losses?' enquired Taff.

'It says the Germans are claiming that RAF losses during July and
August were 1,921. Can't be right, that's the whole RAF and then
some. Our people say the RAF and artillery fire shot down 1,610
German aircraft since the raids on Britain began and that our losses
were 418.'

'Someone's lying,' murmured Oded.

'Typical war propaganda on both sides,' snorted the sergeant, turning the page. 'It says here that 150,000 beds are now empty in our
hospitals – just in case.'

'In case of what?' Taff asked anxiously.

'The invasion, lad. They're coming … It says here that Churchill
expects it to happen by September 15 if it happens at all – and if
Hitler's latest statement to the German people is to be believed.'

Oded saw the terror etched on Taff's face.

'Now what about *this* for bravery?' The sergeant pointed to a photograph of a bombed building. 'A two-storey hospital was bombed yesterday in Kent – doesn't say where. There were many deaths of patients, all women, and several doctors and nurses. The hospital was in ruins but the hospital's Sister, Sister Gantry, crawled down into the ruins and gave morphine to the dying and the injured.'

Taff and Oded nodded in agreement.

'We've got time to listen to *ITMA*', said the sergeant, standing up and brushing down his uniform. 'That Tommy Handley, he's really funny. Helps keep me sane!' He was oblivious to the sly grins on the faces of the other two.

### AT 4.35PM RAF WARREN CALLED. TAFF LOOKED SHOCKED.

'What's happening?' asked the sergeant.

'Two large waves, approximately 380 bombers, with an unspecified number of fighters, are approaching the Thames Estuary. Huw says the likely destination is the London docks but it's unclear how many will peel away to other targets, maybe Bristol. Another formation of twenty-four aircraft has crossed the south coast near Spithead, with Swansea the possible target. The RAF is splitting up this formation as best it can.'

'Christ! 380 bombers? Are you sure you heard right, Taff? That's by far the biggest number yet.'

'Yes, sergeant, that's what Huw said. London's in for a real pasting. We could be too. And that's not all. There're reports that the force has fighter cover of 650 ME-109s – and others.'

For the first time Taff and Oded noticed a crack in the armour of their impermeable NCO. Taff felt sick. This time Oded did fear death.

At 5.18pm the sergeant was the first to detect the drone of aircraft. Taff urgently called RAF Twynells, only to be informed that they were German reconnaissance flights. He queried the earlier report that German raiders had crossed Spithead. The RAF had broken up the formation, came the answer. The raiders had peeled away. The main action was over London, where 250 raiders were hitting London's docks. Other formations were bombing RAF airfields at Kenley and Duxford.

At 6pm Taff called RAF Warren to ask whether the Bristol Channel might be a secondary target. He was told it was only a low probability. In London fires were burning out of control. Whole streets were collapsing into piles of rubble. It was the first day of what ever after would be called the London Blitz.

At 8pm all searchlight batteries on the Bristol Channel were ordered to stay alert, to sweep continuously once darkness fell. RAF Warren reported that more raiders were crossing the English Channel between Dungeness and Beachy Head. The targets were London, and locations in Kent, Sussex and Essex. And possibly South Wales.

By 8.20pm Oded was manning his searchlight, waiting impatiently to switch on. Taff remained close to the telephone. RAF Twynells rang to report that no aircraft had been detected approaching the Bristol Channel, even though the bomber formation reported twenty minutes earlier had split up. The main group was bombing the East End of London – West Ham, Poplar and Stepney were the targets. South of the Thames, Southwark and Bermondsey would also bear the brunt.

'There'll be nothing left of Docklands,' groaned the sergeant. 'God help them.'

'*Blimey, the whole world's on fire!*' was how a London fireman in the midst of the inferno was to describe the devastation and be reported in the national newspapers the following day.

No bombers did target South Wales that night.

### SUNDAY, SEPTEMBER 8, 1940 – DAY 372 OF THE WAR

Despite its losses the previous day, the RAF could report to the War Cabinet at 9am that the following fighters were serviceable: 381 Hurricanes, 197 Spitfires, 50 Blenheims, 23 Defiants and 8 Gloster Gladiators – a total of 697 aircraft were available to defend the country. Three key RAF front-line airfields were out of action: Manston, Hawkinge and Biggin Hill.

Given the extent of the bombing raids over London and the incessant attacks on RAF stations, the War Cabinet urgently met to discuss whether to send out the signal 'Cromwell' – the warning that invasion was imminent. It was decided not to. RAF photo-reconnaissance over the French channel ports showed no unusual movements of the German invasion barges.

The weather forecast for the South West of England was bright sunshine in the early morning, giving way to cloudy conditions for the rest of the day.

*

At 3am raids had been relentless over the whole Greater London area and new waves of bombers were blasting industrial areas of Liverpool and Birmingham. The men of the searchlight battery on the Toll Road were thoroughly exhausted. Their two searchlights, like those of other batteries, had spotted no aircraft. Countless beams on both sides of the Bristol Channel had been scouring the skies. Taff regularly conveyed updates from his mates at RAF Warren and RAF Twynells. Occasionally Oded trained his beam on the still waters of Porlock Bay and on Bossington Beach. Was the beach a possible German landing site?

At 5am the ringing phone had confirmed that all raids throughout the country had ceased. The Luftwaffe bombers and their fighter escorts were returning to their bases. The order was to given to stand down but remain on alert. Britain had been under unremitting attack for nearly twenty-four hours and further raids were expected. Every hope was pinned on the effectiveness of the chain of radar stations. Any formation of gliders with invasion troops should be quickly detected.

Oded collapsed onto his bunk and dozed. Taff stayed on his feet. If he put his head down accumulated tiredness was sure to overwhelm him and he needed to man the phone. The sergeant had gone to another hut to order that breakfast be prepared. Despite the early hour, his lady friend had delivered fresh bread to the battery, and had asked anxiously for news about London. The sergeant had told her what he knew. A farmer interrupted any further conversation as he handed over unsmoked bacon wrapped in old newspaper and a churn of fresh milk. The sergeant thanked them profusely on behalf of his men, ignoring the faces of the young boys peering out from amongst the trees. For two days he had observed them. Today they would have a surprise.

At 6am the wonderful breakfast provided by the locals was gratefully consumed by the men of the unit. When they had eaten, the sergeant had a strange request for the private in charge of the cooking. Puzzled, he carried out a plate of bacon sandwiches to the edge of the wood. From a distance, the sergeant watched as a boy sprinted out and furtively grabbed the plate.

The sargeant then announced that the unit could properly stand down as RAF Warren had confirmed the lack of raider activity, apart from the odd reconnaissance aircraft flying over London and Kent assessing the effectiveness of the previous night's bombing.

This time even Taff collapsed into a sound sleep. At 10am, hearing the sergeant on the telephone, he awoke.

'What's up, sergeant, have I missed anything?'

'No, lad, I needed to call someone in London, in Stepney where I live.'

'Are you concerned about your family?'

'Of course.'

'What's the news?'

'It's bloody awful … terrible. Everything burning and collapsing, bodies everywhere … Stepney, Poplar, the docks … The East End's really copped it.'

'Is your family OK?'

'Mum and Dad spent hours in the underground station – it's the safest place.'

'Have you got brothers or sisters? What about them?'

'Don't have any. Had a sister once. Not now.'

It wasn't the time to pry, Taff felt. He got up and dunked his head in the sink under the cold tap. He needed his wits about him for the day ahead.

'One bloody bomb has been responsible for fifty deaths.'

Taff turned to face the disconsolate NCO.

'Bethnal Green ... not far from Stepney. A Luftwaffe aerial torpedo scored a direct hit on Columbia Market. It's a favourite East End landmark, a large Victorian building with a covered market and shops, and a church and a swimming pool – even a laundry. The Luftwaffe flew so bloody low over south London the residents could see every detail of the aircraft, especially the big black swastikas. People had fled to the old storage area used by the market traders, hoping they'd be safe.'

'What time did this happen, sergeant?'

'Uncertain – sometime late last night or very early this morning. The local hospitals can't cope. The ARP and medical people are still digging out bodies and survivors. Even The London Hospital has been hit by incendiaries.'

'I'm sorry.'

'Make some tea, lad. Don't spare the sugar this time.'

A sense of utter despondency spread among the men of the searchlight battery, a couple of whom were Londoners. What conversation there was quickly died away. No one dared to bring up the subject of invasion.

### At 11.05am RAF Warren called. Huw, too, sounded solemn

'Not, again, Huw, how much more?!' exclaimed Taff as he despairingly noted down that a formation of a hundred raiders, with fighter escort, was coming in over the Thames Estuary. The East End was in for another pounding.

At 12.34pm Taff dashed in to answer the ringing phone. The men were outside trying to spot low-flying reconnaissance aircraft; some were dozing in the sunshine. The RAF station at West Malling in Kent was under heavy attack, reported Huw; some fifty houses nearby were in flames.

'Taff, the invasion has got to be today!' said the excited voice at the other end of the phone. Taff was in no mood to talk.

At 1pm Huw was on the phone again. 'RAF Detling is under

attack!' he gabbled. 'Here in the radar station everyone's saying the invasion is on. I asked my officer but he won't say anything. The place is on tenterhooks. RAF Warren and the whole chain of radar stations in the country are waiting for the codeword, but we haven't had it yet. I shouldn't be telling you this, but we've got standing instructions that, if we're commanded to, we have to burn all our documents and destroy all the key equipment. I'll keep you informed if I hear anything. *You* scared, Taff? *I* bloody well am, mate!' Huw rang off without waiting for the obvious response.

Very slowly Taff replaced the handset. He decided not to relay what he had just heard.

At 1.11pm Huw called again, near panic in his voice. 'The raiders have withdrawn from London, Taff – they're peeling away and going home. What do you think? Are we going to see paratroopers?'

His stomach in knots, Taff went outside to join Oded and the sergeant.

'What did Huw have to say, Taff?' enquired Oded. 'Anything coming our way?'

'Nothing happening, Oded. The raiders over London have gone home, that's all he said. Any chance of a cigarette?'

The breakfast leftovers made an excellent lunch. The unit sat on the grass, many deep in thought, contemplating events that might swiftly unfold. Those with family in London were allowed a phone call home. For one man there was no news. The line was dead and he feared the worst. In the Bristol Channel minesweepers were carrying out their daily duties and a convoy of freighters passed on their way to Cardiff docks.

At 2pm the roar of approaching Merlin engines held everyone's gaze. Flying low down the Bristol Channel into the sun were three Hurricanes in perfect formation, barely skimming the water. Suddenly they banked steeply, split up and flew over Porlock and on to Exmoor.

'They'll be cheering in Porlock High Street. Where would we be without the Hurricane!' The sergeant grinned proudly.

'Sergeant, I have a question,' said Taff.

'Your problem, lad, is that you ask too many bloody questions.'

'What happens to *us* if there is an invasion?'

'We'll be given orders.'

'If the Germans drop paratroops on Bristol and send some of the invasion fleet up the Bristol Channel, do we retreat?'

'No. We stay and fight them.'

'What with, sergeant? Rifles?'

'Shut up, Taff,' Oded interrupted, and added sarcastically, '*Someone* has a plan.'

'Bloody hope so,' pronounced the sergeant. They continued to sit and smoke, competing to blow the most smoke rings.

'Sergeant, I have another question.'

'What now, for pity's sake!'

'Sergeant,' asked Taff, 'are we *really* at war with Germany just because of allegiance to Poland, as Mr Chamberlain's told us? Not so long ago the newspapers couldn't praise Adolf Hitler enough – he's a miracle worker, some of them said, turning round the economy that was in ruins so that now it's far better than ours. I remember seeing photographs of British people shaking hands with the German ambassador, von Ribbentrop – they were all smiling.'

'Now *that's* a really interesting question for a change, Taff. Perhaps our Jewish colleague could provide us with an answer?'

'What?' shouted Oded, jumping up. 'We could be just hours away from invasion, from fighting for our lives, and you blame the Jews for having something to do with all this? You may have the bloody stripes, sergeant, but I don't have to take this. Put me on a charge if you like, but your mind is twisted. Bloody hell, Taff! What have you started now? You and your stupid questions!'

'Calm down, and don't blame our young Welsh friend.' The sergeant spoke casually. 'Isn't it a fact that your people have caused wars for centuries? Jews are the piranhas of the working classes. They live off our backs, always have. You are the money lenders who don't give a damn when penniless families are thrown out into the street. It happens all the time in the East End.'

Oded glowered at Taff. 'Don't even try to calm me down, I've had enough of this Nazi agitprop!'

The sergeant, still seated on the grass, slowly lit another cigarette. Other members of the unit, apart from Taff, shuffled away, keen to stay out of it.

'Can't you handle the truth, Oded? Don't you also know that the Jews were responsible for the Great Plague that swept through Europe in the fourteenth and the seventeenth centuries? At school weren't you taught that the Jewish filth started the cholera epidemics that ravaged Britain in the last century? The Jews are parasites and their influence in politics and the economy is just as contagious. They keep spreading their power.'

Taff was acutely embarrassed about what he had started.

'You're utterly blinkered!' spat out Oded in disgust. 'Perhaps you should be killing Jews rather than fighting Germans.'

The hatred etched on the sergeant's face was unmistakable.

'Taff,' continued an exasperated Oded, 'you ever heard of Kristallnacht? I guess you haven't. Let me enlighten you. Perhaps our NCO here might also care to listen.'

'I *know* about Kristallnacht,' smirked the sergeant.

'Please don't give us *your* version – you listen to *mine*. Taff. It took place mainly during the night of November 9, 1938. *Kristallnacht* means "the night of broken glass". Over seven thousand synagogues and Jewish-owned shops were broken into and many were razed to the ground. Jews, ordinary Germans, many of whom had fought for the German Kaiser in the Great War, were carted away in the middle of the night by SS men and dumped in camps like Dachau. Ever heard of Dachau, Taff? It's a concentration camp in a village near Munich that was famous over the generations for its painters. The prototype camp was built in the early 1930s and it's become the model for a whole series of camps the Nazis have built. There's a similar camp in Austria, near Linz. It's called Mauthausen and it's just as notorious. The prisoners – not just Jews but anyone politically opposed to the Third Reich – are being worked to death in such places.'

'Don't feed Taff such slurs.'

'Sergeant, one day the whole world will wake up to how Hitler and his SS mates have behaved towards anyone who doesn't fit into their Aryan concept of racial and moral superiority. Jews and all those who share any Jewish blood, or their associates, the disabled, the mentally inferior, gypsies, political opponents … they're all being rounded up and taken to these *Konzentrationslager* as the Germans call them. What the conditions in them are like one can't begin to imagine. The trusty Jewish intelligence network is operating in all these conquered lands, sergeant, believe me. Dachau and Mauthausen may just be portents of what is to follow.

'You're in the British army, sergeant. So am I, a Jew. Both Jews and Gentiles ought to know who the enemy is. You're acquainted with the word "patriotism" but clearly you take the side of the Nazis against the persecuted Jews. Would you come to my aid in a fight, protect my back? You'd probably want to pull the trigger.'

'Don't lecture *me* on patriotism! Never question my loyalty to my country!'

Oded flopped onto the grass. He was left with only one course of action. He must request an immediate transfer somewhere – anywhere, but as far away from the sergeant as possible.

Taff passed a cigarette to him. Oded's hands were shaking as he lit it. 'I'm done sergeant, you've beaten me. Just organise a transfer and I'm away.'

'Consider it granted. Let's be rid of you. I'll fix it,' was the hasty response.

If Oded had given up, Taff still had more to say.

'Sergeant, as a Blackshirt you must have participated in the riot at Cable Street? Would I be right?'

'Now that's the best question you've posed this weekend,' interrupted Oded with sarcasm. 'Come on sergeant, enlighten our Swansea grammar school boy here how you stoved in the heads of Jews and Communists in Cable Street. It should be a good tale.'

'You know nothing of what happened at Cable Street,' snarled the sergeant.

'Raw nerve is it, sergeant? I'd be fascinated to know before your SS friends land their gliders and put me and other Jews up against a wall and put a bullet in our brains.'

'Go to hell, both of you!' raged the sergeant. 'Or don't Jews go to hell?'

Oded grabbed the sergeant and pulled him to his feet.

'Oded! Oded, don't hit him! He's deliberately provoking you. You'll be on a fizzer!' Taff shouted.

Unexpectedly, it was the sergeant who backed down, turning on his heel to storm off under the astonished gaze of his unit. He mounted his motorcycle, over-revved the engine and raced away.

'Cable Street … well, Taff, what the hell happened in Cable Street?' mused Oded as the sergeant careered towards the gate.

Just then the Hurricanes reappeared low over the Exmoor horizon, tipping their wings in salute to the men of the searchlight battery before dropping low to return to base at RAF Pembury. The men of the Toll Road searchlight battery waved.

'Stop worrying, Taff,' chided Oded gently. 'The fly-boys will stop the invasion, you mark my words.'

At 4.05pm RAF Warren reported that radar had picked up a large formation assembling in the Calais and Boulogne area. There were up to three hundred aircraft, including significant fighter cover.

The sergeant had yet to return. In the huts the men of the unit anticipated ructions when he did arrive, the worse for wear.

At 5.30pm it was John from RAF Twynells who rang. Raiders were hitting Salisbury and raids were expected imminently over South Wales. London had again come under attack, as had the docks at Dover. The attack on Dover was so intense that twenty-four RAF fighter squadrons had been detailed to intercept the raiders. Some thirty bombers had crossed the coast at Beachy Head and Shoreham, heading for London.

As Taff put down the telephone, the door opened. The sergeant looked rather shamefaced. 'I'm not drunk. I didn't touch a drop,' he said sullenly. 'Taff, you ask too many questions.'

## At 8 pm the news was read solemnly on the BBC

There was no mention of invasion. The nation needed to be put at ease, albeit temporarily. It was reported that 347 German aircraft were lost in the recent raids. On September 7 the Luftwaffe had lost 74 aircraft; the cost to the RAF that day was 27 fighters for the loss of 14 pilots. It was thought that the previous night's raid on London had resulted in 308 deaths and 1,400 serious injuries, though these were only early estimates. The death toll was expected to rise.

'Can't believe those aircraft figures,' said the sergeant, turning off the radio. 'Bloody government imagination. Got a surprise for all the lads … for later.'

He went out to his motorcycle and brought in bottles of Mackeson stout from the two panniers.

'We'll deserve the beer after this weekend is through.'

The searchlight battery was fully geared up for its nightly task, highly efficient as always. Oded and his colleague were waiting to switch on their searchlights as evening slowly rolled into night. Taff was poised by the hut door, ready to dash to the phone which would surely ring, and the other members of the unit were alert to their own important tasks. The sergeant was cool and professional as usual. On the surface it was as if the vicious personal attacks of the day had never taken place. The amity of the unit was as strong as ever.

At the edge of the field, three young lads from Porlock were also apprehensive. They too were exhausted but alert, and prepared for the long night ahead. At home all talk was of invasion but, as observers of the activities of the searchlight battery, they were enjoying the war.

At 8.20pm Taff called RAF Twynells. What had happened to the raiders expected soon after 5.30pm? John replied that the bombing formations had stuck together to hit London and proceeded to catalogue the recent depressing news from in and around the capital. At Dagenham the Ford car works had sustained heavy damage, as had key industrial sites in Greenwich and Wandsworth. The Royal

Dockyard at Woolwich had been gutted. County Hall, The London Hospital, St Thomas's Hospital, the fire station in Whitechapel and a public shelter in Islington were just some of the other targets. London was by now almost paralysed. Wimbledon station had been bombed, and at Victoria a tube train had received a direct hit. Unexploded bombs littered almost every important railway line. In fact, said John, all around the country there had been panic and confusion on an unprecedented scale. Church bells had been ringing to signal the invasion. In Swansea, as one church had started to ring its bells all the others in the town had followed suit, and people had barricaded themselves into their homes and shelters.

Secretly, the War Cabinet met again in its underground bunker for an urgent appraisal. RAF chiefs were again able to assure Churchill that the German invasion barges still had not moved.

*

There was no Nazi invasion that weekend, but September 7-8, 1940 heralded the onset of the London Blitz as the Luftwaffe turned away from the fighter stations to focus on Britain's sparsely defended cities and industrial centres. The death count on the ground in London for that Saturday and Sunday was 650. Total casualties amounted to over two thousand.

On September 14, for the first time, the RAF felt it had gained some measure of ascendancy as it launched unremitting attacks on the amassed German forces in the French ports. Germany's cities were also feeling the reach of RAF bombers.

Hitler, on September 17, informed his generals that Operation Sea Lion (the invasion codename) was temporarily postponed. The German Führer had a far greater prize in mind – the Soviet Union. The scale of that operation would dwarf the conflict seen in Western Europe.

Crippling losses on daylight raids against London, and the Westland aircraft factory in Yeovil on September 30, led the Luftwaffe to revise their strategy and raid mainly at night. The bombing raids across the country in September took a huge toll amongst civilians.

During the month 6,954 died, and nearly eleven thousand were injured. Swansea was attacked three times in September, on the nights of the 11th, 24th and 25th.

But the real horror for Swansea was yet to come.

∗

The Luftwaffe softened up Swansea on the evening of Friday, January 17, 1941. In the bitter cold, with snow lying on the ground, they dropped 178 high-explosive bombs and more than seven thousand incendiaries. The St Thomas area was devastated. In total, 55 died and 97 were seriously injured. When fires were still burning, lighting up the South Wales coastline and marking Swansea as a clear target, the bombers came again at 7.30pm on the following Sunday. The first wave came in low, dropping incendiaries. The grammar school that had stood on Mount Pleasant Hill since 1851 took a direct hit. On the Monday the Luftwaffe attacked again, to finish off what was left of the town. This time its centre was almost obliterated by nine hundred high-explosive bombs, landmines and oil bombs. Not one building was left unscathed. St Mary's church was reduced to a shell and the town's main fire and bus stations were gutted. Churchill was later to visit Swansea, as were the King and Queen, to offer condolences. For many years after the war the bus station bombsite remained as a memorial, a grassed mound where citizens could pay their respects and leave flowers on each anniversary of the raid.

The 'Three-Nights' Blitz' claimed 230 lives, with 397 seriously wounded and more than a thousand others injured. In total, the raids had lasted 13 hours and 48 minutes. Few public buildings remained. Swansea was given a 'breather' until March 3, then the Luftwaffe came again. The last raid of the war was on Tuesday, February 16, 1943. That night 34 died and there were 110 casualties; there was heavy damage throughout the town. Altogether, during the war, Swansea suffered 44 bombing raids.

On the other side of the Bristol Channel, at Minehead, the big gun was fired in anger only a few times. When it was, the crack of it broke surrounding windows, much to the chagrin of local residents. After the war it was taken out but the pier was never put back.

*

On Monday, September 9, 1940, Oded had requested a transfer but declined to specify the reason. The sergeant made no objection; he said he would pass it up the line to headquarters in Taunton. Within a fortnight Oded had gone. He finished the war as a lieutenant in the liberation of Europe that followed D-Day. The army needed his language skills. By April 1945 he was a translator in a special British unit, comprising military intelligence and the secret services, which interrogated captured German officers. Official reports had to be submitted to his senior officers, but Oded also kept his own private notes, recording the names of SS officers and men who had committed unspeakable atrocities against Jews throughout Europe. For much of 1946 he was tasked with travelling to Allied holding camps, including some in Britain, where he attempted to weed out SS officers trying to mask their true murderous identities.

During this time Oded was very much aware of the turmoil in Palestine and the British government's refusal to support an independent state of Israel. The time came to quit the British army. In January 1948 he headed for his spiritual homeland to become an advisor to the Jewish Agency, the political group headed by David Ben-Gurion, which had a military wing fighting British troops in the streets of Jerusalem. After Israel was born in May that year, Oded believed he would be needed in the future conflagrations with Israel's angry neighbours which were likely to occur, but it was decided instead that his interrogation skills would be vital in the ongoing operation to bring Nazi war criminals to justice.

He visited London often as Israel relentlessly pursued those who had worked in the death camps or had been key men within the Third Reich, with responsibility for implementing the Holocaust. Of particular interest to Oded was the whereabouts of Heinrich Müller, the head of the Gestapo. There were German newspaper reports in the 1960s that Müller had died in the ruins of Berlin, but the Israeli, British and American intelligence organisations knew that that trail was false. In reality, the Russians had assisted Müller in his exit from Germany and credible whereabouts included Czechoslovakia and Spain. There had been a price for Russian help in spiriting Müller out of Berlin before the German surrender. In Czechoslovakia, Müller and other key Nazis helped the Soviets train other former Nazis for a substantial spy network in what was to become West Germany. Oded's many pan-European military and intelligence contacts helped him track Müller's well-concealed movements since his last sighting in Berlin in May 1945.

In May 1967 Oded was once again in London for discussions with a key contact in the Foreign Office. The British Embassy in Paraguay had sent them a letter it had received, accompanied by several photographs. Oded gasped when he saw them. The resemblance to Müller was unmistakable. He requested copies. The discovery that Müller was alive left Oded feeling exhilarated. After transmitting the news to Tel Aviv, however, he decided to delay his return by a day. There was another line of enquiry he wanted to pursue – a more personal task.

\*

That afternoon he found himself in London's East End. Blondin Street was a street of terrace houses in Stepney. Oded strolled by No. 11 several times, mulling over the wisdom of raking up past unpleasant memories. There was a café over the road where he sat at an outside table and peered at the broken row of two-up, two-down Victorian houses. The gaps were where bombed homes had been demolished, he surmised.

To his surprise, the front door of No. 11 opened. He immediately recognised the tall man who emerged, his features barely changed over twenty-seven years. Experienced as he was by the nature of his job, Oded felt unprepared as the man strode across the road as if making for the café, but in moments he had passed by – only to stop and gape back at the man who was intently staring at him.

Asserting himself, Oded stood up.

'Stephen?'

'Oded.'

A bus thundered by. Oded offered his hand, a gesture reciprocated with apprehension. A waitress appeared as both men sat down.

'What are *you* doing here?'

'Sightseeing. Thought I'd visit the East End.'

'People don't visit Stepney. There's nothing to see. You're a bit off-course if you want to see the Jewel House at the Tower of London.'

'I wanted to see Cable Street. Isn't that just around the corner?'

'Cable Street? It's a short bus ride away.'

The waitress returned with coffee, which both men stirred in silence, struggling for words.

'Don't worry,' Oded said finally, in an attempt to put his former NCO from the searchlight battery at ease, 'we were in the middle of a war … things get said and are soon forgotten.'

'But you obviously didn't *forgive*. That's why you're here. How did you know I lived in Blondin Street?'

'Looked you up in the telephone directory. Quite simple really.'

The look on the sergeant's face was bewilderment.

'I live in Israel now,' Oded continued swiftly, 'but I've been in London for a few days and I had some spare time. I was curious. The whole area seems to be undergoing regeneration. Was it badly bombed?'

'The East End took so many hits that in some parts whole streets simply disappeared. There was a huge loss of life.'

The conversation again faltered, then he added, 'Were you aware that we have a large synagogue nearby? It was built a few years back.'

'And is there anti-semitism?'

'Barely any.' It was now clear to the sergeant where the conversation was heading.

The two faced each other for the first time since 1940, Oded the skilled inquisitor, the sergeant the unwilling victim. The events of a September long past hung between them.

'But why are you *here* after so many years? What's the point?'

'I said I was curious, and that's no lie. I really did want to see the East End for myself. You have to believe me when I say that I didn't come here to meet you – our meeting has been a complete fluke.'

'Fluke? *You* sitting opposite my house?'

'OK, not quite. I walked twice past your door and I did wonder whether I should ring the bell. Stephen, war changes people. Even bitter enemies can become friends.'

'Isn't it too late for friendship, Oded? I seem to remember that I almost strangled you to death. Why would you want to be forgiving?'

'It's never too late. Do you remember Taff asking you about sin and redemption? Do you think he believed you might change?'

'Oded … there's something I'd like to show you.'

Ten minutes later they were outside a cemetery very close to The London Hospital. The sergeant opened the large ornate gate and beckoned Oded in.

The grave was well tendered. Bending down, the sergeant tenderly rearranged the fresh red roses in the vase under the headstone.

'This is the grave of my sister, Sarah,' he said. 'Have you noted the year of her death?'

'1936 … December 24. She was seventeen years old.'

'Cable Street, Oded … You remember Taff probed me about the battle of Cable Street and I stormed off?'

'What happened?'

'Sarah had a Jewish boyfriend. How ironic was that?'

'I guess that was very unusual in a household with a Blackshirt in the family.' Oded immediately regretted the crass remark.

'You're right. You're so bloody right. If my sister had fallen in love with someone else she would have been alive today. The date was October 4, 1936, a Sunday … it seems as if the nightmare was only yesterday. The Blackshirts, togged out in full uniform, assembled on parade in Royal Mint Court – that butts on to Cable Street. We were to await Mosley and then march through the East End. In Cable Street, Royal Mint Court and the surrounding streets crowds of Jews, Communists, supporters of the Labour Party and other demonstrators had gathered to prevent our march. Bottles rained down on us and the air was thick with spit aimed in our direction. But we didn't react – as per the implicit instructions of the leadership.

'One of the Communists had climbed onto a roof waving a red flag in one hand and the hammer and sickle in the other. The crowd were screaming at him in encouragement. Other demonstrators were shouting, "Go to Germany!" and, "Down with Fascism!" We yelled back, "The Yids, the Yids, we must get rid of the Yids!" That was the signal for the police to wade in, hundreds of them – strangely, not into us, but into the demonstrators. There was utter mayhem before the police managed to gain control.'

'Why did the police protect the Blackshirts? You were Fascists.'

'We weren't the troublemakers. As I said, the Blackshirts had been told not to retaliate. Mosley wanted us to be seen in the newspapers as upright citizens. We'd often pumped out literature saying that the British Union of Fascists always adhered to the law.

'We remained on parade in Royal Mint Court. Mosley still hadn't arrived. Communist sympathisers had used packing cases, cars, even lorries, to block all the surrounding roads. The driver of a London bus had reversed his vehicle across Cable Street. It was an ugly scene. The police were linking arms to keep the demonstrators back. Mosley eventually arrived in his beautiful open-top car and was escorted through the barricades by the police, amongst the uproar. We all cheered but that only made the demonstrators push even harder against the police cordon. More police arrived and the lines held. Mosley remained aloof. He looked immaculate in his uniform – black military-cut jacket, our red-and-white armband on the sleeve, a peaked cap, grey riding breeches – and of course well-polished jackboots. The car very slowly drove up and down our ranks and Mosley, standing up, gave us the fascist salute.'

'How many were you?'

'There were 3,500 of us, men and women of all ages. Yes, we had a large membership of young women. Mosley's car glided by and we saluted him in return. By this time the demonstrators were in a real frenzy. Sir Philip Game, the Commissioner of Police, was escorted by a phalanx of policemen to Mosley's car and there was a heated debate

for well over an hour. The upshot was that Game banned the Black-shirts from marching through the East End but offered Mosley a compromise. Under escort, we could march west, not east, and finish up in Parliament Square. I understand now that Game offered that concession because he thought the number of demonstrators would then be less. To us this was a failure. At Shoreditch, Limehouse, Bow and Bethnal Green, Mosley was meant to have made a major address about how only a fascist revolution could save Britain.

'Eventually at 5 pm, after being on parade for the best part of three hours, we moved off with Mosley grandly at our head. We marched down Tower Hill towards Queen Victoria Street and Blackfriars, with mounted police steering us a path. After what happened in Cable Street and Royal Mint Court the demonstrators tried a new tack to avoid arrest. It was a bizarre spectacle. As we marched onto the Embankment from Blackfriars our long column of Blackshirts was hemmed in by police horses and rows of policemen separating us from silent marching demonstrators on our perimeters.

'It was a peculiar truce that couldn't possibly last. When we passed the City of London School all hell broke out as demonstrators finally pushed through. The police bludgeoned the demonstrators and people fell everywhere. Some were young children who'd accom-panied their parents. Police horses trampled over the fallen. We defended ourselves, and we were no respecters of age. At Temple tube station a huge police presence blocked the Embankment.'

'So, was that the end of the march?' asked Oded.

'Sadly, it wasn't. The Blackshirts were allowed through, the pro-testors were refused – those who tried to get through were beaten up and bundled away by the police.'

'You saw ordinary people who wanted to protest against what you stood for being battered with police truncheons?'

'I did. Many were laid out on the pavements with their heads cracked open.'

'Didn't you feel any sympathy for them?'

'Not at that time, no.'

'Go on.'

'The head of the Blackshirt column reached Waterloo Bridge and there, in front of Big Ben, we were halted by the police for the last time. Mosley's car arrived. He climbed in and raised the fascist salute and was driven off into Westminster. I remember that two days later it was in the newspaper that Mosley had married the socialite Diana Mitford in Berlin, in the office of Joseph Goebbels, the German propaganda minister. Hitler was a guest. That was quite a surprise, I remember.

'Our march was over. Some Blackshirts managed to break through into Whitehall and Trafalgar Square but they were soon overpowered. The violence continued well into the evening.

'Back in the East End, the Communists held a meeting in Shoreditch Town Hall, with loudspeakers in Hoxton Square. That infuriated the Blackshirts and they held a counter-meeting in a street nearby.'

'Did the police protect *you* again?'

'Yes. There were dozens of omnibuses filled with police. They were like locusts.'

'Stephen, I don't yet understand how the events of that day led to your sister's death several months later.'

Tears welled up in the eyes of his former NCO.

'Sarah's Jewish boyfriend … she'd bring him home sometimes. I hated him, but he gave us every courtesy. I refused to talk to him, so did my father. My mother was the only one who welcomed him but she warned Sarah it was unwise bringing the lad into the house because of the Blackshirt support among neighbours. That only encouraged Sarah to keep the relationship going. Once there was an altercation on the front doorstep. Some of my Blackshirt mates came round to see me and bumped into him. They surrounded him and taunted him with names like 'PJ' – our term for 'Pariah Judah'. They wanted to beat him up right there but I stepped in and warned them off. I could see my mother was terrified. My father couldn't care less what happened.

'On the day of the big march, Sunday, I'd stood in front of the mirror in the bathroom and admired my uniform, and practised my salute. It was going to be a very special day for me. I was going to be presented to Mosley by my head of section and given a commendation for my unswerving support of the BUF.'

'"Unswerving support" – what does that imply?'

'I and others would gatecrash meetings held by the Communists. This usually ended in a fracas but I didn't flinch from a fight. It was like a badge of honour. Sometimes we waited outside in the shadows and grabbed one of them. We'd drag him into an alleyway and give him a right kicking. This parade was to be my big day. I'd be singled out to shake the hand of our leader – an honour for any Blackshirt.

'My Dad looked at me proudly when I went downstairs that morning. I stood to attention in front of him and gave him the fascist salute. My mother scuttled away into the kitchen. She disapproved. When I left the house I saw my sister with her boyfriend in the distance, but I thought no more of it. I was so excited I half ran to Royal Mint Court. On the way I was jostled a number of times, even barged off the pavement. My heart was pumping. After the marches of the BUF in Leeds the week before, and at Olympia in London, when there'd been serious trouble, there were calls in Parliament to ban what they called "a quasi-military organisation". Although Mosley ordered that we always had to be seen to abide by the law, he and the leadership were quite happy for us to exercise more strident actions in private.

'Because Mosley arrived late to address the parade, my introduction was abandoned and I was really cut up about it. I made up my mind to make someone pay for my disappointment. Any demonstrator would do, but I'd bide my time. How we grinned when we saw demonstrators being hauled away by the police.

'I wasn't one of the ones that tried to get into Trafalgar Square, but a gang of us did split away at Queen Victoria Street on the return march. It's an area with narrow alleyways, ideal for administering a typical Blackshirt kicking. We found a pub, The Cockpit, behind Old Printing House Square where *The Times* is published. The landlord looked very uneasy when we barged in. There were demonstrators there and we launched into a vicious tirade of "PJ". Pandemonium broke out. A couple of the demonstrators brought out a weapon that was quite common in the East End – a potato with embedded razor blades attached to a piece of string, a viscious thing. We weighed in with our chosen weapon, the standard issue Blackshirt belt. The buckle had been designed so it could be quickly removed, exposing sharp spikes fixed into the leather. We flailed our belts in all directions and didn't care who we whacked. Before the police arrived we'd done a runner.

'I felt elated after that, but I certainly hadn't expected what was in store for me when I got back home. My mother was hysterical. She'd just returned from The London Hospital. In between sobs she told me what had happened. I had no time to change.

'There were several policemen guarding the hospital entrance and when they saw my uniform they barred my way. But I literally begged them to let me pass and finally they relented. The corridors were overflowing with casualties from the demonstrations. I was jeered but I had no energy to fight. I needed to see Sarah.

'As soon as my mother had told me what had happened I'd guessed what had befallen both my sister and her boyfriend. It had been agreed in advance that a small group of Blackshirts, not in uniform, would mingle with the demonstrators with the idea of isolating one or two of them so that they could teach them a lesson. I'd done the same thing myself at the riot at Olympia. Sarah's boyfriend had been one such victim, as had Sarah by association, during the rioting in Cable Street. They were left in a doorway, then were discovered and taken to hospital. The boy had regained consciousness but signs of life in Sarah were erratic and she hadn't come round. My mother had sat next to Sarah's bed for a long time, but the matron gently suggested at last that she go home until the next morning – and pray that her daughter's critical condition improve.

'I found the ward, and the sight of my sister was shocking even to a hardened Blackshirt thug like me. That part of her face not swathed in bandages was twice its normal size. The area round her eyes was badly swollen and I could see by the shape of her jaw that it was dislocated or broken. I broke down and cursed the mindless support I'd given to Mosley and that ranting crony of his, William Joyce. My zeal for the Blackshirts had pushed Sarah further into supporting those who opposed us.

'I called a nurse over to the bed but she kept her distance. Could you blame her, dressed as I was? She told me my sister had a cracked skull, and that her broken ribs might have pierced her lungs. She was barely alive when she'd been carried into The London Hospital. There was only a small chance that Sarah would survive, and if she did she'd probably remain in a coma. I thanked the nurse. She was eager to get away.

'I kissed Sarah on the forehead and walked back past the other badly injured demonstrators who'd put their bodies on the line to halt that stupid march. Propped up in the corridors were old and young men, separated by a generation. Some would have fought in the trenches in the hideous war of 1914-18. Like the nurse they showed contempt at the sight of me. One tried to throw a punch, but I ducked. An old man with his hair matted with dried blood screamed out, "*Why? Why?*"

'God, how I wished I could have turned the clock back and warned Sarah to stay away that day! I couldn't get out of the hospital fast enough, I was in such despair. I reached the police cordon before I realised what I had to do. I stripped off my shirt and tie and threw them away in disgust and then went back in.

'The family of Sarah's lad were around his bedside when I entered the ward. They all turned towards me, an angry bare-chested man in polished jackboots and black trousers with the prominent Blackshirt buckle on his belt. They made a defensive ring around the bed and shouted for help. It stopped me in my tracks. I could only hold my hand up and mouth the words, "I'm so sorry!" Before the nurses could come running I'd left.

'Over the following weeks the doctors gave us some hope, but we knew Sarah's life was ebbing away. She died on Christmas Eve, 1936. She never regained consciousness. The presents on her bed would forever be unopened. My mother and father held hands over Sarah's bed that night, a sign of tenderness I don't think I'd ever witnessed before between my parents. Tragedy had brought them together. Me? I held hands with no one. All I could do was hang my head in shame. I'd quit the Blackshirts. I wasn't the only one. Since Cable Street, all over the country Mosley's followers, disgusted with the violence, had done the same. In Parliament there was an all-party consensus to ban the British Union of Fascists for good. This eventually happened, as you know, in 1940. Up to seven hundred hardliner members were jailed, including Mosley himself. He was released in 1943, but by then his political ambitions were over.

'My quitting gave me problems in the docks where I worked. I was pilloried by my mates. They were die-hard Mosleyites. Many London dockers were. My Dad had been a docker all his working life, mainly in the East India Docks. It was a closed shop. Dockers hated change as much as they hated immigrants. They'd do anything to keep an employment regime that only provided jobs to close family members or vouched-for friends. As soon as I'd left school I'd also became a docker at that yard.'

'I don't understand,' said Oded. 'You lose your sister, beaten up by members of your own organisation, yet your violence towards Jews continued – maybe no longer with a studded belt but through obsessive verbal abuse.'

'You must remember the environment I was brought up in. My fellow dockers hated Jews. My father hated Jews. So did his father before him. In an East End household a son was expected to follow his father. Mosley and his henchmen preyed on all this hatred. William Joyce had us in the palm of his hand. He described Jews as "Oriental sub-men, an incredible species of sub-humanity and a type of sub-human creature". We accepted that. We cheered it.'

'Was that the only reason?'

'No, Oded … No, it wasn't. I did blame myself for Sarah's death but in my confused mind I blamed Sarah's boyfriend even more. As I saw it, Sarah's mind had been polluted by that Jew. This belief became a festering sore. When you arrived at the searchlight battery you were an easy target for all my suppressed resentment.'

'Why did you enlist?'

'I might have been anti-Jewish but I had had enough of the Black-shirts. After I quit the docks I immediately signed up to get away. I did my army training in Yorkshire.'

'You've explained your attitude towards me – your abhorrence of the Jews – but why the hectoring manner towards Taff? What had *he* done wrong?'

'It was as if I was a Blackshirt again. I targeted anyone who was fragile. Taff was too soft-centred, too vulnerable.'

'Yet, somewhere, somehow, Stephen, you have changed – I can see.'

Oded's former NCO said thoughtfully, 'I suppose it was the war that changed me … just as you believe the war changed others. I left the battery in 1942 and after retraining I fought in Italy, alongside mates of all nationalities.'

'Including Jews?'

'Yes … including Jews. I had a Jewish officer. He couldn't have treated his men better. It was a privilege to serve under him.'

The cemetery was by this time deserted. Only the two former foes remained.

'I'm sorry for the way I treated you,' said one softly. 'Will you accept an apology all these years later?'

'It's never too late,' said Oded, accepting the outstretched hand.

'Oded, what news of Taff? Did you ever hear of him after you transferred?'

Oded flinched.

'He's dead, isn't he?'

Oded nodded. 'In my job I have occasional access to British military records. It wasn't difficult to track him down.'

'Where did he die?'

'In Italy. The date of his death is recorded as January 28, 1944. He took part in the first British assault at Anzio. He was in one of the landing craft at Peter Beach.'

'Anzio? I was at that hellhole!'

'It was bad, I understand. There were many British casualties.'

'The landings were fine but we couldn't get off the bloody beach-head. The Germans had one of their huge guns on a railway track nearby – "Anzio Archie" we called it. It kept lobbing shells at us. We had no chance. There was nowhere to hide. We were surrounded by German SS tank units. How did Taff die?'

'He was shot by a German sniper on the breakout from the beach.'

'Do you know what regiment he was in?'

'Your regiment. I also looked into your military file.'

'My regiment? Couldn't have been, I never saw him!' The sergeant was incredulous. 'And what line of business are you in, Oded, that allows you access to such material?'

'I work for government – best leave it at that. Taff must have been one of your new lads. All the regiments that took part at Anzio were reinforced just days before the landings, according to reports.'

'What were the circumstances of his death?'

'Intriguing, according to the written statement of an officer. Taff had given cover to someone from another platoon who was down, and out in the open – his leg had been shattered by a sniper's bullet. Apparently with no regard for his own safety, Taff stepped out from behind the building that was sheltering him and his men and provided covering fire so a medic could rescue the wounded soldier. Taff knocked out one sniper. Sadly he didn't see the second.'

Stephen's knees buckled but he was steadied by a helping hand. Oded felt embarrassed at the distress his revelation had caused.

'That man was *me*, Oded.'

'I know. Your name was in the report.'

'Taff saved my life! And I never knew it!'

'It appears so. That vulnerable grammar-school boy who loved to recite Dylan Thomas, the lad you took pleasure in disparaging – he saved your life.'

The pain etched on Stephen's face was pitiful.

'For centuries Jews have grown a thick skin so that they're immune to verbal abuse,' continued Oded in a gentler tone. 'We've become armour-plated. But the world is full of lads like Taff, nice people who for some reason attract teasing and bullying. They want to fight back but are reluctant to do so, often in the vain hope that the bully might simply change. Taff found his release in an aspiring Welsh poet. Dylan

Thomas gave him the strength to carry on in the face of all your taunts. But that weekend in September 1940 even Taff had had enough. He told me that, in his weekly letter to his mother, he'd written that he wasn't going to take it any more. That's when he began to provoke you, not with his fists or by shouting but with clever questions … questioning your beliefs and your past. He succeeded, too. He made *you* look the fool, the bully, in front of all the men in the battery.'

'So he saved my life – but why?' asked the despondent former NCO.

'As I read the report of his death it became clear that we had both underestimated him – for I had also been short with him at times. As a person he was imbued with a spirit of decency that neither of us was capable of aspiring to. It's possible that Taff deliberately took a bullet for you. There's a chance he might have recognised you, and been prepared to make the ultimate sacrifice trying to save you.'

'Oh Lord, is that in the file?'

'As good as …' Oded felt it unwise to say more.

The report by the officer at Anzio stated that Taff had been extremely brave, but also very foolish. One of Taff's platoon mates called his action suicidal. Moving from cover to stand in the open to take out the sniper was just plain crazy. In more usual circumstances, wrote the officer, an act of such bravery would be posthumously rewarded, but he concluded that such an irrational action should not be encouraged. He recommended that Taff's next of kin simply be informed that he had died bravely in action.

'You never knew about Taff's "quiet place", did you, Stephen? It was a place of solitude for him – a clearing in a strange wood up the Toll Road. I went there a couple of times with him. The conversation between us in this sanctuary was usually about you. I simply hated your guts, and everything you stood for, but Taff for some reason felt inclined to forgive. He saw a different side of you – but then he was very perceptive. He told me he'd enquired about your family in the East End – whether they were safe from the bombing. You'd said something about once having a sister and Taff had observed the pain in your eyes.

'Taff always feared death. He was obsessive about it. He kept a poem about death in his tunic pocket. Somehow it comforted him. I only found it disturbing when he read it to me.'

The early summer's day was nearing its end. The cemetery was deserted but for the souls of the sleeping, the chirping birds and two men who were once enemies on the same side in wartime.

It was time to leave.

As they walked slowly to the cemetery gate, Oded stopped. 'I would like to do something. It's an old Jewish gesture of remembrance.'

Striding back towards the grave, he picked up a small stone nearby and solemnly placed it on top of the headstone. He bowed his head in salute and silently mouthed some words.

'Why, Oded?' asked Stephen over his shoulder, humbly.

'It's what we do. Sarah sounds to me like a brave young woman. She was gravely injured defending her cause, trying to rid London of fascist organisations like yours.'

'I appreciate that act of kindness. Thank you.'

'What happened to you after you were wounded at Anzio? You haven't told me.'

'Didn't my war record say?'

'It told me a bit.'

'I was in hospital in Italy for several months. During my stay I did try to find out the name of the soldier who'd given his life for mine. I'd seen a soldier step out in the open and fire into the building behind me but then I'd lost consciousness as the medic pumped me with morphine before he bravely pulled me away. An officer visited me in hospital to talk about what had happened, but nothing came of it. I always had the feeling that something was being kept from me. So I never did get to discover the soldier's name. I wish now I had persevered.

'I came home on a troop ship and spent time in a convalescence home in Sussex. I was no longer fit to fight. When I was well enough I caught a train to London and returned to Stepney, my home. Few streets had been untouched by the Blitz – the devastation was heart-breaking. But my family's terrace house was still standing and I was welcomed by my mother. Sadly, my father had been killed in 1943 in the Bethnal Green underground station disaster, a shocking wartime episode.

'That happened on March 3. The station platforms were already full – five hundred people were sheltering from an air raid they'd thought was imminent. The sirens were wailing above ground. Unfortunately, another fifteen hundred then began to pile through the station entrance in a panic and in the dim light there was a crush at the top of the stairs. The steps were wet and people began to slip – resulting in a human avalanche. Of the 173 crushed to death that evening, 84 were women and 62 young children.

'You know what, Oded? We lied – the government *lied* about that disaster in the war, and it still lies. Churchill and his War Cabinet never disclosed the full extent of the horror to the public, afraid of the effect it would have on civilian morale. The national newspapers weren't allowed to carry the story. The government couldn't bring itself to admit that the stampede into the underground station was caused not by the air raid sirens but by the intense, unfamiliar noise made by a huge salvo of sixty experimental rockets being fired by the Home Guard artillery unit in nearby Victoria Park, a Z Battery. Even now, in 1967, the silence from the Ministry of Defence is deafening. When it's asked to account for the panic that led to the trampling to death of so many on the stairs it hides behind the previous statement that the sirens were to blame.

'Hogwash, absolute hogwash! By 1943 Londoners were well used to air raids and the drill for entering shelters and tube stations. At Bethnal Green something seriously spooked the people that day. It could only have been the noise of the Z Battery. One survivor later told me the din was petrifying. It's also curious that on that day there was no Luftwaffe raid. So why did the sirens go off in Bethnal Green? Was the operator confused? Did he believe the area was under aerial bombardment? The firing of the experimental rockets was a catastrophic exercise for the local civilians.

'My Dad died that day, crushed to death as he frantically yelled out, trying to stop people tumbling down the steps. When the rescuers got to him they found hardly a bone in his body was left unbroken.

'War changed my Dad, like it did me. When the London Blitz began he immediately signed up as a fire warden, he was so keen to "do his bit". He shouldn't have been in the underground station that day but there'd been a complaint that the fire buckets on the platforms needed filling with sand. So he was there when the huge mob of terrified people stampeded in.

'What is really unnerving are the continuing reports of the blood-curdling screams of women and children, especially when the station is closed in the early hours of the morning. Station staff and cleaners have often claimed to have heard cacophonous cries for help.

'Well, I tried desperately to find a job. I went down to the docks to see what was going, but no new labour was being taken on. The job market was dire and I grew pretty depressed. Like tens of thousands of others, I'd come back from fighting in the war to find there were no jobs and no prospects. Those were grim days.

'But despite the hopelessness there was a real spirit of unity in the East End. People made do. We shared our rations and took care of those who most needed help. The atmosphere was so different from before the war, when the Blackshirts strutted about the old cobbled streets in the misguided belief that only fascism could cure the ills of the world, and intolerant of anyone who differed.

'I did eventually find a job, and in the evenings I helped out in a shelter for the homeless that catered for all religions and national-ities. War is indiscriminate about who suffers.'

'Not strictly true,' interrupted Oded, 'though I understand what you are saying. But some have suffered much more horribly than others. The Jews of Europe were decimated by fascism … I was one of the first officers into Bergen-Belsen.'

'Yes,' said Stephen sombrely, 'I wouldn't disagree with you. Even-tually managing the shelter became a full-time commitment for me and I was able to find some local funding so that we could keep it going. It was our policy never to turn anyone away.

'Do you know what, Oded? That first day I returned to Stepney I had the urge to walk down Cable Street and Royal Mint Court, the centre of so much hatred in October 1936. I found myself walking in the direction of the little alleyway where I knew Sarah and her boyfriend had been set upon by the Blackshirts … I wanted to place some flowers on the place where she'd been beaten near to death. But I was horrified – I couldn't locate it. It had gone in the bombing. I asked a newspaper seller what had happened.

'The raid of September 8, 1940, that great raid on London, had taken it out. That was the weekend when, in the searchlight battery, we were so worried that the invasion was imminent. RAF Warren, you remember, called us to report that 380 plus bombers were heading for London. I remember saying someone was going to cop it this time.'

Oded looked at his watch.

'Sorry Stephen, but I do need to go now. I have a plane to catch to Tel Aviv tomorrow morning and I have a few things still to do.'

Oded shook Stephen's hand. One final act now remained. He took out his wallet and extracted a piece of faded, folded and bloodstained paper. He had found it attached to Taff's military file and had taken it. No one would miss it, he thought. Not now.

He handed it over.

'It's a poem!' said Stephen unfolding it, surprised.

'Yes, the one he always kept in his tunic. He had it at Anzio. I think Taff would want you to have it. He'd have been thrilled about your dedication to the poor in the East End.'

'Shall I read it now?'

'It's somehow appropriate over Sarah's grave.'

Struggling back the tears, Stephen began.

*And death shall have no dominion,*
*Dead men naked they shall be one*
*With the man in the wind and the west moon;*

*When their bones are picked clean and the clean bones gone,*
*They shall have stars at elbow and foot;*
*Though they go mad they shall be sane,*
*Though they sink through the sea they shall rise again;*
*Though lovers be lost love shall not;*
*And death shall have no dominion.*
*And death shall have no dominion.*

*Under the windings of the sea*
*They lying long shall not die windily;*
*Twisting on racks when sinews give away,*
*Strapped to a wheel, yet they shall not break;*
*Faith in their hands shall snap in two,*
*And the unicorn evils run them through;*
*Split all ends up they shan't crack;*
*And death shall have no dominion.*
*And death shall have no dominion.*

*No more gulls cry at their ears*
*Or waves break loud on the seashores;*
*Where blew a flower may a flower no more*
*Lift its head to the blows of the rain;*
*Though they may be mad and dead as nails,*
*Heads of the characters hammer through daisies;*
*Break in the sun till the sun breaks down,*
*And death shall have no dominion.*

'I will treasure this,' he finished, gently refolding the piece of paper.

'Strange poem by Dylan Thomas,' said Oded. 'Taff dreaded dying alone, with no one knowing – yet in war that happens all the time. Many soldiers, airmen and sailors have no known graves. I bet he was keen to get off that assault craft in Anzio pretty quick, given the poem's connection with the sea and his conviction in 1940 that his death would somehow involve water.

'I'm pleased that Taff didn't die alone. The second sniper's bullet lodged in his chest, but he was conscious. When his mates saw him go down, without any thought for their own safety they ran out and dragged him to cover. They cradled his head, lit a cigarette for him and talked to him before he passed away. Taff was a popular and a courageous soldier, the officer wrote in the report. During the year the men in the platoon had been fighting alongside each other, he'd proved his mettle many times under fire. He never shirked danger, never thought twice about helping his mates – even if they did despair that their Welsh colleague kept spouting Dylan Thomas at every opportunity. Every Dylan Thomas poem contains a message, Taff used to say – there were always themes and inner meanings that even men fighting a war could relate to and learn from.'

'Bloody hell, Oded, what a foolish man I've been.'

'Stephen, I really do need to take my leave now. Visiting Cable Street will have to be left for another day.'

'You will come back, Oded? Please.'

'I'd like to … I would *really* like to.'

They shook hands for the final time and parted. As Oded closed the cemetery gate he looked back and saw his former NCO sobbing over Sarah's grave.

✳

Taff had been right about the sergeant, concluded Oded, as he slowly walked away. After he had read Taff's record and made the startling discovery that the soldier he had saved at Anzio, at the cost of his own life, had been the sergeant, curiosity had compelled him to delve further into the sergeant's more recent history. He had called a local newspaper in the East End and was taken aback when the person at the end of the telephone had immediately recognised the name. He was a celebrated character in the East End, Oded was informed, worthy of the MBE he had been awarded for his post-war humanitarian work amongst all faiths in Stepney. Jewish elders in London, said the reporter, had recently bestowed on him an extraordinary award for caring for impoverished Jewish families in his centre for the homeless. At first Oded questioned whether the reporter and he could be talking about the same person. To Oded this man had been a bully and a racial bigot. In the East End he was a hero.

Oded had thanked the reporter for providing him with an address. There was time, he had thought. Surely there was time? He had decided to dely his response to the cable from Tel Aviv ordering him home on the first available flight because war with Israel's neighbours seemed imminent. The Syrians had bombed Israeli villages, provoking retaliation: Soviet-built MIGs were taken out on Syrian airfields. In Egypt, Nasser was massing forces in the Sinai. All reservists, whatever their position, were on imminent call-up.

Nevertheless, it had been the right decision to stay in London.

∗

Oded was busily trying to find a cab when he heard someone calling his name. He turned around to see Stephen urgently gesticulating. 'Please can I buy you a drink, Oded, before you go?' he asked as he breathlessly caught him up.

'It would be a privilege,' replied Oded. Complying with the cable could wait a further day.

At the pub, they toasted an old friend.

'Oded, I listened to a Dylan Thomas play on the BBC in 1954, a few months after his death – *Under Milk Wood*. It was about relationships in a fictitious village in Wales, but there was a recurring theme running through it – a fear of death.'

'Taff would have enjoyed that with his sense of the macabre.'

'The village was called Llareggub,' recalled Stephen, 'but the BBC censors modified it to Llaregyb.'

'Why?'

'If Llareggub is written backwards you get a word with a very different meaning.'

Oded took out his pen and wrote down the letters. 'Taff would have been amused,' he grinned.

'Well, Oded, am *I* still a sinner ... or have I been redeemed?'
Both men laughed. They raised their glasses a second time.

### The searchlight battery

The three brick buildings that compromised the battery used in WW2 remain in the
field near the top of the Toll Road from Porlock Weir to Culbone, now utilised by a
farmer. A resident of West Porlock, a young lad in 1940, still remembers the sergeant
at the battery who chased him and his friends away when they tried as often as
they could to observe the battery's activities.

### The Culbone Stone

For the rest of her life, Margaret Richards argued that she should be given the credit
for the discovery of the Culbone Stone. She married Fred Groves and they ran the
club at Culbone for many years, which is now a popular Exmoor pub.

### Chemical weapons – Brendon Common

There is a 9-ft stone memorial on Brendon Common, a short but difficult walk from
Brendon Two Gates, dedicated to Colonel R.H.Maclaren, OBE, MC who commanded
CW Troops, Royal Engineers, who died on May 20, 1941 after an explosion. At the end
of the war it was necessary to clean up the site used by the chemical weapons troops
on Brendon Common. Nothing now remains apart from the memorial. Visitors beware
– the moor in and around this location is extremely boggy and best left to summer.
Of Larkborough Farm, it was blown apart from artillery fire but remnants of the
outside walls can be seen. Its furniture, cleared out and sold by Jack Edwards,
charged by the military in clearing the moor, is still retained in a
number of Exmoor dwellings.

# Bagging the Bluebird

MAVERICKS HAVE an inability to conform, a characteristic which often leads to confusion, disruption and worse. Such stereotyping had been applied to James Monroe from the very beginning of his police career and it followed him as he became an officer in an elite department of Britain's Special Branch. Yet no one doubted Monroe's abilities, even if he was over-ambitious and cavalier in some of his actions. Monroe had single-handedly tried to bag the Bluebird – such a stupid plan. Now he was serving his penance, a punishment that had to date lasted for five years. Often he felt like resigning – jacking it in, moving on – but each time he held his tongue and hoped that he would return to the role he had been trained for, and which he excelled in. Such resolve is a distinctive quality of a maverick.

The official complaint from an outraged Russian ambassador to the Foreign Office had acutely embarrassed the government, MI5 and Monroe's bosses at Special Branch. They had had no option but to transfer their young officer to one of the most tedious duties in the department – checking the movement of illegal aliens at the three terminals at Heathrow airport. In Moscow how the Bluebird must have laughed.

*

Monroe had left university in 1962. Most of his fellow graduates joined merchant banks in the City of London in pursuit of riches, or entered other lucrative professions. Monroe embarked on a less traditional path. The Metropolitan Police had launched a 'fast-track' programme for new graduates, with attractive promises that looked

117

highly alluring on paper. Time 'on the beat' would be reduced to a minimum and early advancement was guaranteed providing reports were good. Forever game for a challenge, Monroe signed up the day after the end of his finals. In the pub he had announced to his fellow students, with drunken bravado, that *he* would be doing something *really different* with his life.

His father, a retired army officer, didn't think much of that decision; neither did his mother, or anyone else that knew him. But he filled in the forms, attended the interviews and passed the medical, and within the month he found himself in uniform at the Met training college.

No one was surprised when Monroe passed out top of his intake. The reports were glowing. But the examining officers who signed them knew that Monroe was far too clever to be a copper – and that that would be his downfall. Such reasoning might have been behind his posting to a police station in south London, a backwater where the conviction rate for serious crimes was barely half the national average – hardly the place for a new recruit with ambition. Too smart by half was also the view of the station inspector, who had little time for a copper with a decent education. He had come up through the well-attended university of life and a degree, in his opinion, was no indication of the qualities necessary for a copper on a London street. Initially dispirited, Monroe willed himself to make a good fist of his first appointment.

All he needed was a break.

*

The two plain-clothes officers who visited the station didn't cast a glance in the direction of Monroe as they were ushered into the office of the inspector. As a junior constable, and the only university man, it usually fell to Monroe to make the tea. This day was no exception. He knocked on the inspector's door before going in with the tray and the conversation paused. No one thanked him.

Monroe and another rookie were later summoned. There was an important job to be done, stated the inspector blandly. His visitors earlier in the day had been from Special Branch. They had requested assistance as their resources were fully deployed elsewhere. A local villain needed to be watched. It would be a passive surveillance, involving merely keeping a record of anyone who entered or left the large Victorian house in quite a smart tree-lined street on their patch.

The surveillance was pure tedium, as the inspector had jokingly predicted. Worse still for Monroe, and much to the annoyance of his girlfriend, he was assigned the night shifts.

It was on the third day that events took a dramatic twist, shortly after Monroe had taken over the watch. A man furtively approached the house, carrying a briefcase, head down. Reaching the covered porch, he rang the bell. Monroe watched through his binoculars, his heart racing, as the door opened and the visitor hurried in. Anything unusual needed to be radioed in immediately, but Monroe hesitated. He needed to be sure about just *who* he had seen. When the visitor later departed, Monroe left his unmarked vehicle and walked towards him, pretending to be searching for a house number. The middle-aged man passed, clearly anxious to leave the area. Monroe now felt certain, but still he didn't call the station. He had other plans.

From a phone box, after he had handed over to his colleague in the morning, he called Special Branch. Within the hour he was in the Charles II Street headquarters. But self-congratulation turned to dismay when he was given a roasting for ignoring procedure. A thoroughly miserable Monroe was told to report back to his police station. The surveillance was henceforth terminated. When he arrived, he was met by an apoplectic inspector who had been subjected to a similar ear-bashing.

Normal routine was resumed for Monroe. He walked his beat, nicking tearaways and shoplifters. Three months later the *London Evening News* reported, under a banner headline, that a junior government minister had been arrested for providing favours to members of London's gangland in return for cash. He pleaded in mitigation that he had been compromised after explicit photographs had been taken of him cavorting in a dingy hotel room with two male escorts. A glowing parliamentary career was at an end and a jail sentence loomed. On the strength of the news, Monroe was taken to the pub by his colleagues to celebrate. Even the inspector put in an appearance and bought a round.

The following day, as a badly hung-over Monroe reported for work, the desk sergeant beckoned him over for a quiet word. 'There may be some unexpected good tidings coming your way, lad,' he said with a wink.

'Special Branch appear to have forgiven you, constable Monroe,' explained the inspector later. 'They want to make use of your skills – they've requested your immediate transfer to Charles II Street, and it's been granted. I understand you're to become a "birdwatcher".' He was gratified that a rookie in his charge should have caught the eye of the organisation every copper aspired to join. Monroe was ecstatic, though unclear about what 'birdwatcher' meant. The inspector had been unable to enlighten him.

*

Every summer the Russian Intelligence Services and MI5 play spy games with each other over British Council places allocated to young Russians keen to undertake postgraduate studies in Britain, usually to learn English. It is normal for the KGB to attempt to place fledgling recruits on the list for consideration. MI5 weeds most of them out, but some fledglings do get through. They arrive in Britain with every intention of completing their courses. The 'birdwatchers' of MI5 and Special Branch await them, and it is rare for 'targets' not to be 'bagged'. One fledgling who tried to thwart the birdwatchers was Stanley Lekarev, a recruit of considerable talent from a family that included several renowned Russian actors and actresses. And this Russian indeed had acting skills that would not sully the family reputation.

MI5 had given Lekarev the codename 'Bluebird' – a reference to the speed machine Donald Campbell was racing on Scottish lochs in search of a new world speed record. The Russian Bluebird, like his namesake, was fleet of foot. He was always on the move, bird-watchers reported, combining studying at Leeds University with many of the recreational pursuits typically enjoyed in higher education. His careful movements, however, suggested that he had been well schooled by his Moscow masters.

Leeds University was a popular choice among Russian students. It was radical – the student protest was loud against the Vietnam War and American and British foreign policy in general. But protest was one activity the Bluebird stringently avoided, despite pressure from his fellow postgraduates. One professor in the English faculty was of particular interest to British Intelligence. A Communist activist, he would invite students to discrete drinking parties to gauge their political sympathies. The Bluebird received several such invitations. He went, once, but was warned by the Russian Embassy in London never to go again.

After six months MI5 handed over their records of surveillance to Special Branch – a standard procedure. They were convinced that the Russian worked for the KGB, despite the lack of any evidence. There was every likelihood that he was in the SVR, the KGB's elite international intelligence department, undergoing 'seasoning' in the country where he would eventually serve as a political attaché in the embassy. That would be his cover.

Monroe was assigned as sole birdwatcher and he relished his first real chance to show his talents. He was determined to find proof where MI5 had failed. In the first weeks of his surveillance Monroe followed, more or less, the pattern of his predecessors, and he logged tedious reports to London.

As the days lengthened into spring, he marvelled at the Bluebird's prowess on the university tennis courts. It was a popular decision to make him team captain in the forthcoming inter-university championship. Leeds proved unbeatable, especially the team's Russian captain who won every singles match he played, excelling also in the doubles. Celebrating afterwards, the captain was never short of a pint of beer in his hand from an admirer or team mate. Monroe noted in his log that, while the other students succumbed to their drink, the

Bluebird could hold his. London informed him that KGB officers are taught how to drink hard yet remain capable.

This was one very clever spy, reflected Monroe.

*

Cambridge had been formidable opponents in the tennis championship but the Leeds captain had come through, as he always did, in a stirring final match, winning handsomely in the singles. Sitting in his car, watching the clubhouse as both teams later socialised, Monroe perused his log for the week. He had never before followed the Bluebird to an away fixture – there hadn't seemed to be much point – but Cambridge was a city with many attractions to ease the boredom.

When the Leeds coach driver pulled up the captain ushered his team and a happy group of spectators aboard before settling down in the front passenger seat.

To Monroe's surprise the coach took a different route to Yorkshire on its return journey. Instead of joining the A14 north, it went south-west to Royston, passing through the villages of Meldreth and Melbourn before it stopped in a busy lay-by near Bassingbourn. The doors opened and some of the occupants jumped down and raced to the bushes to relieve themselves – including the Bluebird.

Monroe slowly drove past but as he did so his ear drums were almost shattered by the overhead roar of jet engines. He watched with schoolboy fascination as the undercarriage of the bomber seemed almost to scrape the hedgerows as it touched down on an airfield close to the road.

Monroe mulled over why the coach should have diverted. The following day, posing as a university administrator, Monroe had a chat with the driver. How had the tennis gone in Cambridge? Fine, he was told, despite a detour which made them very late getting back to Leeds. Casually, Monroe asked why he had taken an alternative route. It wasn't unusual, said the driver. The expression on his face was deadpan. The captain always took his camera and often asked for scenic tours of East Anglia and other parts of the

country. That revelation was enough to send Monroe immediately to London.

Before his curious Special Branch colleagues he pinned up on the squad notice board the largest map of the UK he could find, on which he had ringed every location visited by the Leeds tennis team since the beginning of the inter-university tournament. Next to this map he positioned another, sourced from the Ministry of Defence, which identified all RAF, USAF and other military installations, including top-secret armament manufacturing sites. His MOD contact had also supplied a report on the strategic capabilities of RAF Bassingbourn: it was a front-line station that flew Canberra bombers whose two squadrons were trained to deliver the H-bomb. Extra fuel tanks had been fitted on an armed Canberra which remained on 24-hour standby – Quick Reaction Alert – for bombing operations beyond NATO borders in Europe.

Held in particularly high regard by the Air Ministry was the squadron equipped with the latest PR-7 model. Under its fuselage was housed advanced photo-reconnaissance equipment unequalled in any other country. These aircraft and their pilots supplemented another Canberra PR-7 squadron based at RAF Laarbruch in north Germany, which was undertaking covert reconnaissance missions across East German airspace, flying under the Soviet radar and barely above ground level. Several had been shot down by Russian fighters, reported the MOD – events that for obvious reasons were always hushed up.

The correlation between Monroe's markings on the two maps was obvious and his conclusions rolled further up the line to MI5.

A couple of days later Monroe and an experienced colleague were inside the Bluebird's meticulously tidy room while the Russian was away at a two-hour seminar. As his associate began his methodical search, Monroe sat on the bed and gazed around. Photographs of university tennis triumphs adorned the back of the door – but to Monroe one looked oddly out of place. He had studied the Bluebird's file umpteen times. Stanley Lekarev was aged twenty-six, the British Council application had revealed. In the two-year period since his graduation in Moscow he had been employed in Leningrad at a research centre. Its precise nature was not revealed. The Bluebird's organisation – no doubt a KGB front – had counter-signed the application. Monroe had smiled ironically when he had seen the final approval from the British Council – the decision that the British taxpayer would provide funding.

The room was 'clean', as Monroe had expected that it would be. No codebooks were hidden under a loose floorboard or taped beneath the tatty wardrobe. But it was only a matter of time, he thought ... soon the mask would slip.

∗

Back in London, Monroe had his photograph developed. He had taken it when his colleague had gone down the corridor to the communal toilet to check that nothing had been concealed in the cistern. He made a call to a contact in MI6 – a relationship that had been developing in recent months. Aware of Monroe's reputation as a maverick, the Secret Intelligence Service had encouraged the Special Branch officer to share any information with them if he thought it helpful. Monroe was about to stretch that relationship a bit further.

While MI5 and Special Branch were deliberating on how best to deal with the Bluebird, Monroe was transferred to other surveillance duties. A fortnight later he received a private phone call and was asked to meet the caller in the Red Lion in Duke of York Street, off St James's Square. The pub was heaving as Monroe eased himself through the throng, into the quieter back room. His contact was already at the table, his head buried in an evening newspaper with a screaming front-page headline announcing that Harold Wilson's bankrupt Labour government was to go cap-in-hand to the International Monetary Fund to seek an immediate loan of £500 million to partially fund the chronic balance of payments deficit. The waiting pint was welcome.

'I thought Harold promised he'd save us from those spendthrift Tories,' exclaimed Monroe loudly.

'All the bloody same, these politicians – full of flannel and little else. Not an ounce of sense between them,' grunted the MI6 man, putting the paper down.

'You are to be congratulated.' He smiled, placing Monroe's photograph on the table. It showed two men in tennis gear posing with their rackets. The older man looked fit and athletic for his age. Behind the Russians was the dreary-looking entrance to what looked like a football stadium.

'General Alexsandr Mikhailovich Korotkov, known to his friends and colleagues as "Sasha" – the head of the First Chief Directorate of the KGB who experienced a rather sudden death,' said the MI6 contact, pointing to the solemn older man, who looked unhappy about having his picture taken. 'Korotkov had an exceptional CV in international espionage – not bad for someone who started his KGB career as a junior lift engineer in the Lubyanka. Someone obviously saw the untapped potential in him. He was sent for special training. Thereafter his career blossomed. Arguably his greatest success was to "turn" some four hundred German POWs imprisoned in Russia and leak them back into the new West Germany – by all accounts a phenomenal operation. To this day the West German government is utterly compromised. Photographs of Korotkov are extremely rare, given his position within the KGB, and *you* managed to obtain one. But what are the Bluebird and Korotkov doing with tennis rackets outside a football stadium you may ask?'

'You're going to tell me?'

'The stadium belongs to Moscow Dynamo, Russia's premier club, but it isn't only the game of football that's played inside. The KGB's tennis courts are there, where the top brass meet once a week for a game and a drink. Some young officers are invited – such as the Bluebird. They are all very able tennis players. They are expected to display their strengths, but promotion prospects might be compromised if they didn't occasionally lose to their seniors. I am led to understand that, before the Bluebird came to Britain, he was captain of the KGB tennis team that played regularly against opposition but under the guise of a fictitious government institute. For the Bluebird to have played tennis with the likes of Korotkov, he must obviously have been marked out for a promising career. I did say, though, that Korotkov had died suddenly. Apparently he collapsed on the tennis court in this very stadium – from a heart attack. The KGB had lost one of their top men.'

'No wonder the Bluebird had the photograph in his room – but he took a chance with it. That was out of character for our man,' commented Monroe, who was now ready for his second pint. He wanted to celebrate. Yet again one of his hunches had proved invaluable. He bought whisky chasers.

'Cheers, my friend. You found something that MI5 didn't.' The MI6 man raised his glass.

'Where do we go from here?'

'Without telling Special Branch and MI5 about the photograph – otherwise you'll be in big trouble – we'll let them know that well-sourced information has been received in Moscow that a British-Council-funded postgraduate at a British university is a KGB officer … and we'll give them the name.'

'And me?'

'I guess you'll continue as you are. Obviously surveillance suits your talents.'

'What will happen to the photograph?'

'*I'll* take it,' said the MI6 officer.

They finished their drinks and left. For Monroe all thoughts of success dissipated as yet again he had done the legwork for others to take the credit.

MI5 and Special Branch agreed that surveillance of the Bluebird should recommence, and that Monroe should continue as bird-watcher. The Russian would be leaving the country at the end of his course but further observation could uncover his contacts. The university term was now over but the Bluebird remained in Leeds, researching in the library for his due essays and only occasionally venturing out into the nightlife of the city. Monroe's logs to London became tiresome reads, if anyone cared to study them.

But the maverick would live up to his deserved reputation.

*

'Mad' was how Monroe would jokingly describe it many times later as his career went from strength to strength. The anonymous note he left in the Bluebird's pigeon-hole at the university suggested that he was the tutor of two very bright female undergraduates sympathetic to the Soviet Union who would like to travel to Moscow to meet fellow students if finance could be arranged. He felt uncomfortable about providing his name, he wrote in the note, but he did give a working local telephone number and suggested that they meet to discuss the matter. If the Russian did respond, Monroe decided, he would seek permission to develop the operation further.

The note was taken, but there was no call from the Bluebird. The only call was from Monroe's office. It was an angry instruction for him to return and justify his actions.

The Bluebird had indeed read the note. Although his initial reaction had been one of interest, he felt inclined to contact the KGB station at the London Embassy for advice. Smelling an MI5 set-up, the senior officer decided that there was political capital to be made. The ambassador could use an imminent meeting with the British Foreign Office to cause maximum embarrassment. A thoroughly outraged Foreign Office soon fingered James Monroe as the architect of the Leeds caper.

Blame attached to MI5 as well as Special Branch, but whereas the former demanded the immediate dismissal of Monroe the latter stood by its man, even if he had been naive in believing his plan might flush out the Russian. Sacking was considered but Monroe was spared that ultimate sanction, though there would be a penance in addition to the scolding reprimand. Monroe was given the chore that Special Branch officers go to great lengths to avoid. Weekend rosters needed to be filled in at Harwich, a popular entrance point for illicit members of the Russian Intelligence Services, and at Heathrow, where it was necessary to check for illegal alien entry. At least twice a month Monroe's name would be inked in.

\*

Sunday evening, August 18, 1968 was unusually quiet at Heathrow's Terminal 1. An hour before the Aeroflot flight from Moscow was due, Monroe had wandered into the deserted staff canteen for coffee, and to study the passenger list. Earlier in the day there had been some excitement. Colin Bland, the Rhodesian cricketer, had arrived and his entry into the UK had been barred. He was left hanging around the terminal under escort, awaiting a return flight to Salisbury.

The majority of the Moscow passengers on the passenger manifest were returning Britons. Most were salesmen who slogged their way around the capitals of Eastern Europe, attempting to sell expensive capitalist luxuries to cash-strapped, state-run Communist enterprises. But the list that evening included a group of Russian students. Monroe smiled and gritted his teeth. The Bluebird episode some years earlier had left him still feeling raw. He strolled down to the arrival gate and, as the last passengers trooped away to Immigration, Monroe remained to catch the crew – especially the good-looking Aeroflot air hostesses. It was the only consolation of weekends on duty. He lit a cigarette but didn't have to wait long. Two pilots appeared first, chatting excitedly at the prospect of a night in London.

Today something was different. There were two extra crew members compared with the usual tally. Monroe attempted to scrutinise every face, but they were tightly grouped together, almost as if they were forming a protective human shield. At the centre were two of the male stewards, in step with their colleagues but with heads bowed. Taking an alternative route, Monroe raced to Immigration. Soon the Russians arrived and their banter hadn't dissipated, the captain engaging in good humour with the woman from passport control manning the crew channel. One by one they were waved through. The two at the rear were quiet and thoughtful as they presented their passports.

Monroe's stomach turned over. His nemesis had returned, instantly recognisable despite the moustache and trendy sideburns.

After counting the crew boarding their minibus, Monroe rapidly returned to the Special Branch office in the Queen's administrative building and grabbed the phone. The MI5 duty officer calmly took the call from his opposite number at Special Branch in Charles II Street, enquiring whether its man at Heathrow could be mistaken. He listened carefully to the measured response before offering his thanks and calling the deputy head of counter-intelligence, whom he knew would be at home that evening Special Branch was already tailing the coach to the London hotel, close to the West London Air Terminal, where all Aeroflot crews stay over. At Heathrow Monroe was instructed to remain until the end of his shift.

*

In the morning there was a discernible buzz on the Director's floor at MI5 headquarters. His two secretaries had been in since the early hours, gathering together papers for the urgent meeting that had been called. Several members of MI6 would be attending, including its newly-appointed head, John Rennie. The venue was Ryder Court, on the corner of Ryder Street, a favourite MI6 location since the 1940s and now, during the Cold War, a debriefing centre for Russian defectors. Around the oval table were placed copies of every MI5 and Special Branch report on the Bluebird while at Leeds, the report on Monroe and his ill-advised scheme that had brought ambassadorial wrath on the British Intelligence Services, the MI5 dossier on a former political attaché at the Russian Embassy in London, and details, where known, of each Aeroflot crew member.

The Bluebird's reappearance was a concern, but it was the identity of the other KGB officer masquerading as a member of the flight crew that had led to the frantic calls to the MI6 station at the British Embassy in Moscow. Why was the KGB's top spymaster now working undercover in Britain?

The MI5 file on Vladimir Barkovsky was thick. As a prominent member of a select group assigned directly by Stalin during the war to steal British and American nuclear secrets, Barkovsky had penetrated many of the research establishments and university departments in Oxford, Cambridge, Birmingham, Liverpool, Edinburgh and London – centres that had developed working plans, without American assistance, to build thirty-four atomic bombs. When ready, in 1943, they could have obliterated Berlin, Munich and many other German cities.

The spymaster had not been seen in England since 1948. Then, for some unknown reason, he had returned to Moscow in a hurry after his stint as second political attaché. After postings to the Russian Embassy in Washington and the New York Consulate, where he had run spy rings at Los Alamos and at the special nuclear research laboratory at the University of California, Barkovsky now worked in the Lubyanka. He was deputy director of the STI, the Science and Technology Intelligence Department, one of the two key departments within the KGB. With the rank of colonel, Barkovsky was responsible for managing all Russian agents in the West who provided military, scientific and industrial intelligence.

Rennie and his MI6 colleagues had read their own even bulkier file on Barkovsky before they arrived at Ryder Court. Included in it were the names of ten top physicists and chemists, several renowned in their respective fields, whom MI6 had been convinced were wartime traitors, though MI5 in their wisdom had never brought them to book. In Oxford one such Russian cell included several German scientist émigrés at the Clarendon Laboratory who passed over not just atomic intelligence but also the secrets of radar, a British invention. This university city was so leaky that the Clarendon became an intelligence goldmine for the Russians. Only in the years after the war, as spies were gradually uncovered or denounced by defectors, was Barkovsky named as a major wartime Soviet controller.

There was one agent in particular whom MI6 wanted to see prosecuted for his treachery. That was the physicist codenamed 'Moor' whom Barkovsky would meet in the tea-room at Moor Street railway station in Birmingham. Seconded by the Clarendon to head a team working on membrane separation in a converted theatre on an ICI site, Moor had handed over to Barkovsky the results of secret experiments to separate uranium on an industrial scale. This process was the very essence of atomic bomb manufacture; it was the forerunner of the process eventually used by the Americans to build the Hiroshima and Nagasaki bombs.

As Special Branch continued to monitor the hotel in West London, the meeting in Ryder Court began. Photographs of Barkovsky and the Bluebird were projected onto a large screen. That such officers were in the country in disguise could lead to only one conclusion, said the MI5 chief. It must be a covert operation of the highest importance for the operational chief of the STI to be personally involved.

At Ryder Court it was agreed that a team of birdwatchers, with back-up where necessary, should be employed to conduct surveillance once Barkovsky and the Bluebird emerged from the hotel. MI5 fiercely objected to Rennie's suggestion that the birdwatchers be a combined four-man MI5 and Special Branch team which included James Monroe because of his familiarity with Stanley Lekarev. The issue was hotly debated but Rennie got his way. However, he agreed that the two MI5 birdwatchers should have ultimate responsibility. As the meeting closed, Rennie silently hoped that the maverick would live up to his reputation.

In West London the Aeroflot crew left the hotel for the airport, but without their two bogus members. For the birdwatchers, events were about to take a turn for the worse.

*

That night a large group of revellers gathered in the hotel bar. Russian students from a number of London colleges had readily accepted the offer of free drinks at an impromptu party hosted by the embassy. There was a lively atmosphere as the students sang, danced and discussed events in Paris, London and other European capitals. Revolution was in the air all over Western Europe as police fought running battles with angry students. Outside the hotel the birdwatchers could only look on in dismay at this diversionary tactic. Some twenty black cabs were ordered at the end of the evening, courtesy of the Russian Embassy, all timed to arrive together. There was pandemonium. The senior MI5 birdwatcher reluctantly reported that Barkovsky and the Bluebird had probably slipped away, destination unknown.

Rennie's hunch about Monroe was quickly put to the test and it was Monroe's hunch that provided the first lead. In desperation, he had phoned a contact in Leeds, someone whose name had not been mentioned in any of his surveillance reports three years earlier.

Lekarev had been in touch by telephone, as he said he would be the next time he was in England, Monroe was informed quietly. If there was time the Russian hoped to get to Leeds to see old friends, but he couldn't promise. Monroe gently probed further. Had Lekarev indicated where he was going? He had mentioned Bristol, came the response, as the receiver was slowly replaced on its cradle.

Monroe and his three colleagues quickly drove to Paddington station in the hope that a train was the preferred means of transport. One train was already slowly pulling out for Bristol Temple Meads. The two MI5 men raced across the station concourse, yelling instructions to their fellow birdwatchers, before precariously scrambling aboard. Walking slowly back to the departures board, Monroe noted that one further train would run to Bristol that night.

They sat in the tatty bar, its atmosphere smoky and fetid from mouldy carpets and stale beer. It gave them a wide but discrete view of the concourse. At 11.40pm two men joined the queue at the ticket office. 'Welcome back my old friend,' Monroe whispered to himself, 'I've missed you.' He reported in his news. After that he made another call, out of earshot of Harry Tate, his Special Branch colleague.

As the train pulled into Bristol in the early hours of the morning the surveillance operation was in full swing. Monroe and Tate were among the first group of weary passengers to get off the train. The Russians were some distance behind them. Outside the station the red Vauxhall Viva pulled away from the curb with the Bluebird at the wheel, and Monroe and Tate followed in their car, a discreet distance behind. Ahead, somewhere, was the MI5 team.

Soon the bright street lighting of Bristol was behind them as the Russians headed south, the two cars of the birdwatchers interspersing with other vehicles driven by experienced Bristol-based Special Branch officers. Darkness turned into daylight; it would be a beautiful morning.

After several halts, when the Russians either stretched their legs or consulted a road map, the car stopped on the A39 to Minehead, at the petrol station in West Quantoxhead. As the attendant filled up the car he happily answered the Russians' questions and pointed towards the coast. The Bluebird pushed money into the attendant's hand and offered grateful thanks before speeding away. Moments later Monroe and Tate pulled up and Monroe flashed his ID card. He radioed his colleagues and London control with the name he was given – that of a civil servant who had recently retired to East Quantoxhead. A friendly type, the attendant had said.

For generations the cliffs of East Quantoxhead had been enjoyed by locals as a favoured promontory from which to view the Bristol Channel. Monroe saw the Viva parked by the duck pond, without its occupants. The MI5 men had already witnessed what had happened. The Russians had located the cottage with the large red door. They had knocked several times, but its occupant was either not at home or felt disinclined to answer. Giving up, they had taken the path to the sea. Monroe and Tate followed another route. Through his binoculars Monroe could see Lekarev attempting to skim pebbles over the water, and Barkovsky laughing at his lack of success.

'What's going on?' whispered Monroe to his colleague. Tate could only shrug. In his thirty years of service he'd never been on an operation quite so bizarre.

After an hour of idling along the beach, the Russians returned to the duck pond to find an old Landrover parked. Barkovsky knocked again on the red door. He knocked twice more before the retired major opened it slightly to view his unwelcome callers. It was wide enough for the Bluebird to wedge his foot in the opening and barge in, closely followed by Barkovsky.

The senior MI5 man urgently contacted control for instructions. After what seemed like a very long time his radio crackled; he listened intently, then raised an immediate and vociferous objection. But the order stood. He was briefed on what was in the major's MI5 file and told to share the information with Monroe and Tate. Monroe was fascinated.

✻

In the early 1930s, in the maelstrom of Manchuria, the resident of this ancient whitewashed cottage had been a young man seeking his fortune in China, chasing export opportunities for Britain's largest cigarette company. British companies were in the vanguard of this thriving commercial market, selling anything from aircraft to household goods – and plentiful cigarettes – to a grateful population. The drinking clubs in the cities were low dens where the beer flowed and the prostitutes enjoyed rich and easy pickings.

China was becoming a fertile recruiting ground for Joe Stalin. Like other Britons, the subject had been targeted by the NKVD, the predecessor of the KGB, which maintained a training centre in Manchuria staffed by a large contingent of intelligence officers. Mixing freely with the westerners were Russian talent-spotters who ingratiated themselves by offering free drinks and a variety of personal services.

At the time there was much speculation about the increasing Japanese threat, and hostility turned into full invasion in 1932. Manchuria was annexed as the Japanese army unleashed its terror machine of torture, rape and indescribable slaughter on the Chinese population. It was time for the cigarette salesman to return home. The once booming economy had collapsed, though the bank account of this commercial traveller was well into credit, thanks to a large financial inducement offered in return for his promise to supply intelligence once he was back in Britain and in the employ of either the military or the Civil Service. His covert income would supplement his regular salary in London. A 'friendly' source within the Ministry of Defence helped provide the opening, just as the clouds of war were gathering over Europe.

By July 1941 Russia was under German assault and the ambitious former salesman had been promoted to the rank of major in Defence Intelligence, the counter-intelligence arm of the Ministry of Defence that worked closely with MI6, MI5 and other wartime agencies. He had been provided with a new Russian codename – 'Agent D' – and such was his value that Stalin himself received copies of documents that were passed to Moscow via the London network. To Stalin, who had his own independent intelligence service based at the Kremlin – Strategic Intelligence – the importance of 'Agent D' as a spy ranked

as high as 'Scott', another British agent, an academic, who worked
first in army intelligence and then as a government advisor on Soviet
affairs in the Foreign Office, with access to the highest category of
restricted material. The major and Christopher Hill were more
important to Stalin than even Kim Philby, Donald Maclean, Anthony
Blunt and John Cairncross. Philby had long been suspected by the
Russians of being a double agent, but there was no doubting
the loyalty of 'Agent D'. As a result he was very well paid for the
services he provided.

The British learned of the existence of 'Agent D' only when a
senior KGB officer defected to the Americans in 1962. They left him
*in situ* at the government department for which he was then working but carefully monitored his contacts. Further agents might be
exposed. The major's contact with his controller, reported the defector, had abruptly ceased in 1948. Further surveillance on the target
by MI5 yielded nothing of value and, rather than risk the embarrassment of a public trial, it was decided to discontinue the operation.
The major was moved to a series of low-key departments that offered
no scope for advancement and it was no surprise when he took early
retirement.

⋆

The Russians left East Quantoxhead after two hours, and the
surveillance restarted. Back-up cars waiting on the A39 were alerted.
Monroe and Tate remained behind, on the instructions of the reluctant senior birdwatcher. It was now Monroe's turn to knock on the
red door. When it opened the Special Branch men stated their names
and offered identification.

'Major, for two hours you have entertained two members of the
KGB. We would very much like to know why,' said Monroe firmly,
fixing a glare on the worried face in front of him. He noticed the
tremble in the major's hands as he gripped the door.

The former MOD counter-intelligence expert, once held in great
esteem by Stalin, crumpled. Monroe didn't wait for an invitation to
enter. He manoeuvred the pathetic figure into the living room and

pushed him unceremoniously into a chair. As Tate began his metic-
ulous search of the house, from his jacket pocket Monroe extracted
two photographs.

'This man is KGB captain Stanislav Lekarev,' he stated, pointing
to the Bluebird. 'The other is Colonel Vladimir Barkovsky. Yesterday
they entered this country from Moscow – apparently to see you.
Kindly explain.'

'Don't start making threats to me, Monroe,' came the steely
response from the major. He was now sitting up stiffly, more
composed.

'Let me make myself very clear, major – or perhaps I should call
you 'Agent D'. I've been instructed to warn you that, if you do not
co-operate, your life as you presently know it will be in shreds. You
will undergo a public trial and you will go to jail for the rest of your
life – though the life of a prisoner convicted of treason can be very
short, I understand.'

' I haven't the faintest idea what you're whittering on about! I want
you and your colleague, who judging from the noise upstairs is
pulling apart my possessions, out of my house *now* or I'll call the
police.'

'The police? Do you really think they'll shelter you from your
crimes? You used to work in Defence Intelligence so you must be
familiar with our alternative procedure. What you don't tell *me* will
only be wrung out of you in another place, where pain is easily
administered and your protests will go unheard. We know you have
been complicit with the Russian Intelligence Services since your
recruitment in China in 1932. Your betrayal of this country is exten-
sively documented.'

The major dropped his head into his hands. It looked as though
he was about to burst into tears. The man's a wreck, thought
Monroe.

'Stalin's spies don't cry, major. I thought you'd be made of sterner
stuff. Do we talk or do I hand you over to someone who knows how
to inject some very dodgy substances?'

Upstairs Tate was still banging about.

'Sounds like Harry's dismantling your furniture, major. He's very thorough, you know – comes of a long career searching the premises of KGB agents. Will he find anything?'

The major glared at him defiantly. 'Of course he'll find nothing, as you know full well,' he sneered.

'My feeling too, major, but Harry's got to go through the motions. He'll be starting on downstairs soon. Shall we try again? Your Russian friends … Where are they heading? Hurry – please – with your answer.'

'Exmoor. Clicket. Near Timberscombe. About twenty miles away.'

Monroe pulled out his radio and called it in. 'You're not lying to me, major, I trust? Are we talking about a village? I've never heard of the place, neither have my colleagues.'

'You'll need to get to Clicket before the Russians do. I'll say no more,' responded the major, almost inaudibly.

Monroe tarried. Determining where the Russians were going had been the precise instruction from the senior birdwatcher, but there were other demands. They had come from another source. That was the only reason he hadn't quit his soulless job at Heathrow, checking passenger manifests for Special Branch. A prospective lifeline had been offered.

With Harry now busying himself up in the attic, Monroe pushed on, despite the risk.

'I haven't finished with you major. Was this an unexpected visit?'

'Can I have a drink?'

'Of course, major, let me pour you a whisky.'

'I was a fool, a bloody stupid fool,' admitted the major. 'Yes, I was recruited in China, but then so were many others.'

'But you were not an idealist, major. You handed over our secrets in return for money. That gave you a comfortable lifestyle and probably bought this place.'

'Can I offer you a Scotch, Monroe?'

'Spare me the hospitality. I need to know about your relationship with your two KGB friends. Why were they here? For what purpose?'

'They threatened me.'

Monroe sighed. Harry would soon be coming downstairs. 'I don't have much time and I don't care two hoots if they did. Why have they come from Moscow to see you?'

'It was 1948 … June. I came across a document in the Ministry of Defence.'

'*What* document?'

'A copy of a top secret memo. I can't remember the contents.'

'Stop playing games. What was in it?'

The major lowered his eyes.

'It must have been important,' said Monroe, 'something *really* special, for a top KGB officer to track you down twenty years later. Are they here to find it?'

The expression on the major's face confirmed that this was the truth.

Monroe repeated the question: 'Barkovsky and Lekarev are here to find this memo – that's it, isn't it?'

'Work it out for yourself Monroe.'

'Let me think this through further, major. At the MOD in White-hall you came across a top secret memo. You stole it but you didn't deliver it to your Russian masters in 1948. And now Moscow desperately needs it after twenty years. Am I making sense?'

'Yes! Damn you, Monroe, that *is* what happened. The loss of the document was discovered before I was able to leave the building. The place was in uproar, security people swarming all over the place. I couldn't even return it. I stuffed the thing into my shirt and joined in the hue and cry. As I was in Defence Intelligence I took it upon myself to interrogate the female secretaries who'd had access to the Minister's private papers.'

'That's rich!' snorted Monroe. 'Who'd you get to take the blame?'

'No one was directly blamed. One secretary was dismissed for negligence.'

'How come *you* had access to this memo?'

'I don't want to incriminate anyone else … Not now.'

'You had an *accomplice* who had access?'

The major looked embarrassed. 'I had a friend … a special friend.'

'Do I presume a male friend?'

'Yes. In the Civil Service you get dismissed for being homosexual. Out of the office we had to meet in secret. It was usually in a downstairs bar near Tottenham Court Road. There were others ... like us.'

'I've no comment to make on your personal life, major – but this boyfriend of yours obviously worked closely with the Minister of Defence and stole documents for you? Did you tell him you worked for the Russians? But that's irrelevant right at this moment. You still haven't told me what's in the bloody thing that warrants Russia's top spymaster coming to England.'

'You'll have to get to it before the Russians and read it for yourself. I'm not telling you,' said the major doggedly.

'Are you telling me that the copy of the memo is somewhere in Clicket? Did you deposit it there?'

'As I've told you, I couldn't return it. It was too dangerous. On other occasions I took documents out of the MOD building and in the evenings I met my controller, usually in a cinema in Notting Hill. He'd take them away to photograph at the embassy, then pass them back to me in the cinema later. I was always able to return the documents in the morning. But this time I was in a real panic. In the days following the loss staff were being randomly searched. I assumed that even I was under suspicion, maybe even under surveillance. MI5 is brilliant at that kind of thing, as you know. The night I took the memo I called a number from a busy phone box in Soho – the emergency number my controller had given me. I told him what was in the memo. It was late, but we arranged to meet that night.'

'Do I rightly assume you didn't turn up?'

'What a perceptive Special Branch officer you are, Monroe.'

'Skip the sarcasm. So why didn't you show?'

'The memo was dynamite. I knew that the Russians had to have it. They had every right to see it. But for the first time I realised the level of risk I was taking. There couldn't have been many copies made of the original. For all I knew the copy sent to the Minister of Defence might have been the only one. Surely, I thought, MI5 would interrogate everyone in the paper chain, including my friend. So there and then, outside the cinema, waiting for my controller, I bottled it. I walked away. I didn't show for any subsequent pre-arranged meeting either.'

'What did you do with the memo?'

'It was clear I couldn't easily return it, or even deposit it somewhere in the MOD building where it could be found. There were prying eyes everywhere. MI5 had countless meetings in the building with Defence Intelligence, including myself. Fortunately I was able to protect my source by offering to interrogate him myself. We had decided not to see each other out of working hours whilst the flak was flying.'

'Why didn't you just destroy it – get rid of the thing?'

'I should have done that immediately, but I didn't. I felt I had to keep it … just in case. Strange, I know, but that was what I thought at the time. I hid it in Clicket. I'm a regular walker and every year, I'd do the coastal path trail that starts in Minehead and runs west. Another walker had told me about Clicket so I reconnoitred it. I needed to find a place that I felt certain no one would discover.'

'You've told the Russians where it is?'

The major nodded.

'So I have to get to it before the Russians do.'

'You do. But be warned. If you *do* find it your chiefs will not allow you to read it.'

'Why? What's the big secret?'

'If you want the memo that badly *you* find it, *you* read it.'

'In Clicket …'

'Yes.'

'Buried?'

'Maybe.'

'No clues? Can I assume you were more co-operative with your Russian friends? I've a good mind to take you with us,' said Monroe as he heard Harry on the landing.

· 'I'm too old now. And *you* will need good boots – it's down in a valley.'

Tate came into the room and shook his head. 'Clean upstairs and in the attic,' he reported to Monroe. 'Shall I start down here?'

'Don't waste your time, Harry. I hardly think that one of Stalin's highly-prized assets would leave incriminating evidence lying around. Turns out, Harry, that the major here is a bit of a squirrel. He buries things.'

Harry looked puzzled.

'I'll fill you in later,' grunted Monroe derisively, just as the doorbell rang. The major's hands started to tremble again.

'Major, your escort … People want to talk to you. Harry, please let them in.'

'Who are they?' remonstrated the major. 'I thought I was co-operating?'

Three MI5 minders entered the room, the no-nonsense sort, short on courtesy and long on rougher qualities. Two pinioned the major's arms whilst the third yanked his head sharply back, prising open his mouth and checking every tooth.

'What are you looking for? Is that necessary?' asked Monroe, concerned.

'Poison,' replied one. 'A concealed phial that's bitten into and releases whatever the KGB is now using for its agents.'

'Where am I going? Monroe, please stop this!' the major pleaded.

'I don't know,' shrugged Monroe, 'but I'm sure you'll be made comfortable, wherever it is.' The minders liked the joke. That was the cue for the major finally to break down. He sobbed uncontrollably.

'Major, before Harry and I take our leave, tell me one thing. Was Barkovsky your London controller in 1948?' The one-time cigarette salesman nodded pathetically.

'You know, Harry, I'm beginning to feel a bit sorry for the major,' said Monroe, as he watched the man being strip-searched, blind-folded and handcuffed before being dragged out to the waiting car for the long drive to London. Harry was unresponsive. Nothing felt good about what he had just witnessed.

Monroe made two calls as Harry retired into the fresh air for a cigarette. The first was to the MI5 birdwatchers, the second to a private number in London. The voice at the end of the phone was specific: 'Find it,' was the instruction, 'before MI5.'

Before Monroe left, he walked about the house trying to understand why people – especially those in privileged positions – betray their country. 'The lure of money always wins,' he muttered under his breath. He slammed the red door behind him and smiled at the group of curious villagers who had gathered around the duck pond.

The chase was on.

*

Monroe and Tate drove away, stopping again at the garage on the A39, this time to ask for directions to Timberscombe. As for Clicket, the attendant could only offer apologies and shake his head. An hour later the Special Branch birdwatchers drove into Timberscombe and parked alongside their MI5 colleagues near the school.

The Russians, said the senior MI5 man, were at the Lion Inn nearby. 'It appears they've booked into the pub for the night. Go over again what the major told you, Monroe, and leave nothing out.'

Monroe sensed the mood, as did Tate. Both had wondered why one of the MI5 officers had not remained behind in East Quantoxhead to interrogate the major. Nagging questions had plagued Monroe's mind on the drive to Timberscombe, thoughts he had declined to share with Harry. For the first time Monroe had an inkling that he might just be a pawn in a far bigger, much murkier game.

'There's nothing more to add to what I told you on the phone,' said Monroe. 'He stole a document in 1948 and hid it somewhere down a valley in this Clicket. The Russians know that too. That's why Barkovsky's come back – to claim it.'

'That's all? And it was twenty years ago?'

'He may say more when your people soften him up.'

'Too late by then.'

'Have you located Clicket?' asked Monroe, attempting to change the course of the conversation.

'Not yet, but someone in this village must know. It certainly isn't on our map. Are you sure you weren't mistaken?'

'I didn't trust the major an inch, but if we've been misled then so have the Russians if they're staying overnight at the Lion. *We'll* need somewhere to stay.'

'I'll make some enquiries,' offered Harry, eager to escape from the prickly atmosphere between the birdwatchers that had suffused this operation from the beginning.

'And I'll take a look round the village, talk to some villagers. Might be useful,' said Monroe eagerly. The MI5 men glanced at each other before the senior man nodded his consent.

Monroe sat in his car and pondered their options. He saw a road sign to Luxborough and took the road, admiring the view of the valley below. Coming across a farm, he pulled into the drive. The farmer seemed impressed when Monroe showed his credentials and he was invited in. Two mugs of cider later, a precise drawing of the location of Clicket, and of two entrances into the 'lost' hamlet in the valley bottom, was in his pocket.

The easiest way down was from the other side of the valley, the farmer had insisted – the easterly route. There was no signpost but the track to the side of the deserted farm building was difficult to miss. Clicket, which had literally dropped off the map, was a long-abandoned collection of decaying dwellings dotted on either bank of the brook and hidden in the trees. Its inhabitants had scraped a living processing lime from a quarry and selling flour from the mill. Life had been desperately hard. By the 1850s just six families had remained and the last was gone by 1900, taken by the bitterly cold winters of the late 1890s and bouts of diphtheria which ravaged Exmoor. The stone and thatch properties had gradually collapsed, leaving only the creeping ivy and the ghosts of generations past.

Jubilant, Monroe returned to Timberscombe. Harry had managed to rent a room, despite the misgivings of the house owner who felt uncomfortable at the disclosure that four men without luggage were to share it. She asked their business and was politely informed that it was a police matter: under no circumstances was their presence to be disclosed to anyone. She scurried away, murmuring that a hot supper and local ale would be available – an offer that was soon readily accepted.

The Russians were in no hurry in the morning. They leisurely consumed their full English breakfast and revelled in the attentions of the landlord, who was delighted to be entertaining his first visitors from the Soviet Union. At dinner the landlord had provided brandies on the house and the Bluebird had stood, glass in hand, toasting all and sundry in the bar in perfect English; even the usually reserved Barkovsky joined in. Through a window Monroe had observed the spectacle, wondering what the landlord would say if he knew one of his guests was Russia's top spymaster. He'd dine out on the revelation ever after.

At breakfast the landlord gave Lekarev a map showing the exact location of Clicket, and the easterly route down to it favoured by locals on pheasant shoots, when beaters would move through the wood and chase out the birds for the guns.

In their room the birdwatchers had spent a far less comfortable night, disturbed by the frequent changing of surveillance shifts, but a hearty breakfast raised their spirits. They discussed how best this new day should unfold. There were problems: how to follow the Vauxhall Viva inconspicuously down the narrow lanes, and the weak reception on the portable radios, given the rolling terrain.

The plan was to split their resources with Monroe readily agreeing to the suggestion that the MI5 men should cover the northerly route into the valley, the one Monroe had suggested as the most likely of the two entrances the KGB officers would take. The Special Branch men were ordered to cover the other side of the valley – the easterly route – in the unlikely event that backup should be necessary. Harry Tate asked whether the Russians would be arrested. It was an MI5 operation from now on, he was informed bluntly. Monroe merely looked on.

*

By 10am the Vauxhall was on the move, the landlord directing his guests from the car park and waving the Russians away. The MI5 birdwatchers had already left the village; their vehicle was parked out of sight on the Luxborough road. Through their binoculars they had scoured the valley and spotted the stile that marked the entrance to the dense woodland. They cursed that their radios were barely registering a signal.

Monroe and Tate were positioned on the other side of the valley and had the deserted farm building in their sights. Monroe's heart skipped a beat when the Vauxhall slowly rolled into the track from the road, the silhouettes of the occupants picked out by the sun.

'My nemesis is drawing ever closer,' whispered a transfixed Monroe to Harry. The adrenalin was pumping.

The car doors slowly opened and the Russians cautiously moved towards the building. It was empty, just as the pub landlord had said it would be. They followed the deep tractor ruts to the gate that led into the steep rutted field. Words were exchanged before a reluctant Barkovsky returned to the vehicle. The Bluebird was soon out of sight.

Despite his age, Tate was the first to reach the Vauxhall. He wrenched open the passenger door and dragged out a stunned Barkovsky, clamping a large hand over the Russian's face before he could yell out.

'I have diplomatic immunity,' spluttered the breathless KGB spymaster when Tate finally pulled his hand away.

'And then what? Return to Moscow – job done – with a document in your baggage?'

'I know nothing of any document,' Barkovsky replied, with a cavalier wave of his hand. 'I demand you allow me to immediately call the Russian ambassador. I repeat, I have diplomatic immunity.'

'We heard,' jibed Monroe. He set off in the direction of the Bluebird but turned back with an urgent request for Tate. This was accepted by his colleague, but not before he had strongly voiced his disapproval and concern.

Monroe set off again, mulling over in his mind how a 'lost' village on Exmoor came to hold a twenty-year-old secret vital to the intelligence services of both Britain and the Soviet Union. At the gate he saw the Bluebird entering the wood at the valley bottom. That man is *really* fit, reflected Monroe, not relishing the difficult descent down the track. With every moment now critical, he ran for all he was worth, cursing his own lack of condition and his liking for a pint.

His lungs heaving, Monroe flung himself to the ground as he reached the wood's perimeter and crawled into the undergrowth. He could see little in the unwelcome blackness. The wood was quiet, apart from the gentle sound of running water somewhere deep inside. Monroe stealthily creapt forward, in the knowledge that the brook would lead him to the village. He cursed as dry twigs snapped noisily under his weight. Soon he could discern the shapes of buildings whose inhabitants were long gone. There was a movement. The Bluebird was progressing from dwelling to dwelling, flicking over the rubble of lime-rendered stones. In one collapsed building the Russian scrabbled furiously among the ivy and moss undergrowth. He was cursing.

Monroe had noticed a large building, one that resembled a mill, on the other side of the brook, its walls more or less intact. The Bluebird was now striding purposefully towards it, across the bridge. Monroe crossed the brook further down and circled back to observe him. Half buried in the moss at the base of the mill was the millstone. Very carefully the Russian slid his hand underneath, following its contour, until he discovered what he had come from Moscow to find – the package that hopefully contained the document so urgently needed by the Russian premier, Nikita Khrushchev. He had ordered that the chairman of the KGB should personally instigate this operation.

Gently extracting the well-wrapped package, the Bluebird excitedly brushed off the accumulated dirt and uttered a muffled triumphal cry in Russian. He took a pace back to congratulate himself. This must surely be the pinnacle of his SVR career, surpassing even his debriefing of the defector Kim Philby which had provided the first evidence that the MI6 defector might after all be a double agent. In Philby's closely guarded Moscow apartment there had been

several moments, when both men were drunk, when he had encouraged an off-guard Philby to suggest that in his Cambridge days he
might have been encouraged by British Intelligence to sign up
with one of the two Russian talent-spotters who had infiltrated the
debating societies at Oxford and Cambridge. He had subsequently
suggested to his KGB chief that he take Philby on a week's holiday to

Prague, in an attempt to find out more. It would be Philby's first trip outside Russia and it carried a high risk of assassination by the CIA, but Stanley Lekarev had quickly gained a reputation within the KGB for his unconventional methods. His maverick ideas were not to the liking of everyone within the corridors of the Lubyanka.

✷

Barkovsky had desperately wanted to be with him in the valley, but the spy chief had felt that the steep climb down would be too much for him. That was a bitter disappointment as Khrushchev had personally requested Barkovsky's presence at his dacha to emphasise why it was so imperative to locate the document. Over the last twenty-four hours, and particulary the previous evening in the pub in Timberscombe, Barkovsky had explained more of what had occurred in June 1948.

Barkovsky's 'Agent D' had excitedly called him about a memo he had acquired with sensational contents that needed to be passed to Moscow as soon as possible. He had given Barkovsky some details and had arranged to meet him that evening at the cinema, the usual meeting place, but had not showed up. Returning to the embassy, Barkovsky had told the basement cipher room to send an urgent message directly to General Fedotov, the head of his department in the Lubyanka. Fedotov cabled back, insisting that Barkovsky make every attempt to contact his man. Comrade Stalin had been informed about the memo and had convened an urgent meeting of the Politburo. Barkovsky carefully worded daily advertisements in the personal column of *The Daily Telegraph* – one way embassy controllers used to contact their agents – but the emergency phone line remained silent. All Barkovsky could say to Moscow was that he was still trying. That the major had been compromised was a definite possibility, but as he was observed arriving at and departing from the MOD each day that conclusion was soon discounted. Nothing appeared unusual in his demeanour. He did not carry his briefcase in his left hand – the warning signal to Russian watchers that all was not well, and they should stay well away.

To everyone's surprise, a month later, 'Agent D' did communicate by phone. There had been another memo, he said, along the lines of the first but with more detail. That news was immediately transmitted to Moscow and a return cable reported that the Englishman was to be awarded the Order of the Red Banner on the direct orders of Stalin. It was a matter of the utmost importance that contact be re-established with 'Agent D', ordered Fedotov. But yet again the major had failed to appear at an agreed meeting place in Kew Gardens.

Only yesterday, in East Quantoxhead, had Barkovsky belatedly pinned the highest award for an intelligence officer on the pullover of the reluctant recipient whose retirement had been rudely disturbed by a past he had tried hard to forget. In return, Barkovsky demanded information. It was not readily forthcoming.

*

Tentatively, Monroe crawled forwards. Events were about to take an unimaginable twist. The maverick was to meet his nemesis, a man with a similar penchant for operating outside the normal boundaries of intelligence when the need arose. Aspects of what was about to take place in Clicket were to remain a secret between them for life.

'Hello, my British friend,' called out the Bluebird, without turning around. 'I've been expecting you. What took you so long?'

Monroe froze.

'Come out,' said the Russian. 'There's no point in hiding any more.'

Monroe emerged from the undergrowth, dusting himself down.

'I have to compliment you, Mr James Monroe.'

'You know my name?'

'After your unfortunate escapade in Leeds your name was given to us by the Russian ambassador in London. He demanded it from your embarrassed Foreign Office. We threatened to go public with the story – to one of our friends in Fleet Street – if the British didn't offer a full apology. And they did. In Moscow I drank to your misfortune.'

'So why pay me the compliment?'

'When I was studying in Leeds I knew I must have been under surveillance, but never once did I spot a watcher. You are good, James Monroe, very good. At the KGB training school in Moscow we had regular lectures from operational officers with international experience on how to avoid detection, and how to pick out a tail. In a sense I was the failure, not you.'

'How could you *possibly* know that it was me who was tailing you now?'

'I was against the Aeroflot idea from the outset. It was too high risk in my opinion. Using another route into Britain was my choice, but Barkovsky was in charge and he chose the airport. It was obvious that, if we were seen, you would be a birdwatcher, given your past experience with me. What *did* alert your people at Heathrow?'

'The crew size. There were two too many; it deviated from the norm. I picked it up immediately.'

'You were on duty at the airport?'

'It's been my penance for what you call my "unfortunate escapade". I should have been sacked but I was kept on. Someone must have had some faith in me.'

Lekarev laughed. 'What delicious irony is that! Even worse, we led you straight to the major.'

'You did, but it appears we've known about your chum for years. Please pass over what you have in your hand,' beckoned Monroe firmly. 'We will then rejoin your colleague.'

'Do you know what is in this package?' asked the Bluebird in a hushed tone.

'Do you?'

'I have some idea. But you hold all the cards. Arrest me. Take the package. But aren't you even slightly curious about what it contains? I have a feeling that you aren't alone – so you have little time to consider.'

Monroe was certainly inquisitive, but it was highly likely that his MI5 colleagues would come crashing through the wood at any minute. He hoped that Harry had bought him some time, as he had asked, by not contacting the other birdwatchers with the news that Barkovsky was being held and that he was on the trail of the Bluebird.

'Well my British friend ... your call. Are we to discover the secret which the British government is desperate never to reveal, and which Khrushchev wants to use against his Cold War enemies?'

'Do I get your word that you will never reveal that I allowed you to open it?'

'Would you trust the word of a KGB officer?'

'I have a strange feeling that I can.'

'Our secret remains here with us. Shall I open the package?'

'Go ahead ... but be quick, very quick,' replied Monroe nervously, deciding that he would tell MI5 that the Russian got to the package first and broke the wrapping.

The Bluebird sat on the millstone and carefully undid the binding as the seconds ticked ominously by. There was a deathly silence in the wood. Only the gurgle of the brook pervaded the stillness. From layers of protective packaging the Russian managed tantalisingly to tease out two unmarked manilla envelopes.

'There are *two* documents!' he exclaimed.

Very odd, thought Monroe. The major had mentioned only one.

'Let's read the bloody things together,' said Monroe suddenly, pushing the Russian aside. This will look good, he shuddered. How could he ever explain to MI5 why he was sitting on a millstone next to a serving KGB officer, reading documents that were clearly marked 'Read and Destroy', the highest security classification? His career would be ingloriously at an end.

The first memo was dated June 26, 1948. It was addressed to Clement Atlee, then prime minister, and its sender was the head of MI6, Major-General Sir Stewart Menzies. A source, wrote Menzies, a reliable contact in the US Department of State in Washington and a trusted friend of Britain, even if the Truman Administration generally wasn't, had disclosed to him personally that security in recent days at US airfields in Britain was at its highest level since World War Two. That had been confirmed, said Menzies, by MI6 officers who had, over a period of two weeks, observed large transports arriving from the US. Their contents were unloaded and kept in closely-guarded hangers. Menzies referred to this operation as "Chevalier". Only a few outside the White House were in the loop. Menzies concluded that he hoped to have more information shortly.

'Quickly ... quickly,' said Monroe impatiently, 'go on to the second document.'

'This one is dated July, 26, 1948 – a month later. Again it's from Menzies to Atlee.'

Monroe wasn't listening, he was struggling to digest what could herald Armageddon – the great symbolical battlefield of the Apocalypse, the final struggle between good and evil. The hairs on the back of his neck stood on end and his throat was dry.

Fleets of US bombers, flying from US bases in Britain and West Germany, were to unleash 133 atomic bombs on 70 cities and towns in the USSR, with Moscow the target for eight of the bombs on one day alone. Operation Chevalier, Truman believed, would obliterate Communism from the face of the earth for good. The United States would then be the only superpower, free to expand its doctrine to every country in the world without military hindrance. In World War Three there could be only one victor.

Yet this ultimate battle of the nations may not be over so easily. It was possible, said Menzies, that despite the onslaught Stalin might not sue for peace. He might abandon the wrecked cities west of the Urals and move east – the same ploy the Soviet premier had used to Russia's advantage in late 1941 when the SS and the Wehrmacht besieged Leningrad and were within a day's march of the Kremlin in Moscow. One Truman adviser even forecast that the war might last for two years, given the size of the country.

There was an even grimmer remedy. The remaining nuclear arsenal of America – some two hundred bombs – would complete the final annihilation. In Operation Fleetwood, President Harry Truman would achieve the vision of Adolf Hitler, who repeatedly ranted to his adoring German nation that Bolshevism would be 'wiped off the face of the earth' Aircraft based in the Pacific would complement the aerial bombardment and cities east of the Urals would burn. In this total war, stated Menzies, the loss of life would run into tens of millions.

Menzies' memo included extensive footnotes specifying key targets, the first, at Arzamas, well to the east of Moscow and south-west of Gorki, necessitating one entire battle attack. In the environs of Arzamas was a research and production facility codenamed 'Arzamas-16'. There an atomic bomb was nearing completion. It lacked only the 6 kg of plutonium at its core. The second location destined for oblivion was a compound at Chelyabinsk, even further east, that was perfecting this vital ingredient. A former school for Spanish children in Obninsk, sixty miles south-west of Moscow and codenamed 'Laboratory No. 5', was the third of the ten targets on Truman's list. The school was now the home, and its eight laboratories the workplace, of Dr Heinz Pose and thirty-three other German physicists who had been captured by the Russians in the final weeks of the war. There was a race against the British and Americans to locate scientists who had worked on the German nuclear project. It can never ever become public knowledge, stated Menzies to Atlee, that behind the RAF and USAAF firebombing of Dresden in January 1945 was the need to destroy an SS industrial facility in the woods outside the city. The Russians had got Pose, who shared with them Hitler's blueprint, that had been so near to fruition in Dresden, for an atomic 'superbomb' which could have changed the result of the war.

In conclusion, Menzies warned Atlee about the likely level of fall-out and its spread: it would contaminate large areas outside the USSR. 'I am no expert in this matter,' wrote Menzies 'but in my opinion Western Europe might also become a nuclear wasteland uninhabitable for generations. America, no doubt, would be safe.'

Both men sat on the millstone, neither offering any immediate comment.

Monroe was the first to break the silence. 'Why *didn't* it happen? What stopped it in 1948? This was designed as a preventative strike

– it was obvious Russia was more advanced than we had thought and was building its own bomb.'

'That is a conundrum,' replied the Russian. 'We are security officers, not politicians or generals. I do have a theory, though.'

'Go on.'

'Berlin … it was all to do with Berlin and the Soviet blockade. That was finally lifted but no one really knows why Stalin agreeed to the American demands.'

'I can buy that … but for that theory to be correct Truman could never have publicly announced this nuclear option.'

'Carry on, James Monroe. I believe that you and I might be arriving at a similar conclusion.'

'It had to be done in such a way that Stalin accepted that Truman's plan was genuine – and nothing better than a stolen document. If the Soviets covertly obtained the details of Operation Chevalier and Operation Fleetwood, Stalin would see that confronting Britain and America over Berlin would be catastrophic for the Soviet Union.'

'I agree. But there's more …' encouraged the Russian with a wave of his hand.

'There is indeed. That implies that we were aware of "Agent D" long before your Russian defector fingered him. The unwitting major was used as a disinformation channel in 1948 – and maybe even for the duration of the war – by *us*. The major was the conduit to Barkovsky, who was duped even though "Agent D" had lost his bottle and didn't show up with the memos. He had said enough on the phone. That must have scared the living daylights out of Barkovsky – and Stalin, when he read the Barkovsky ciphers from London.'

'That's my conclusion, too, my British friend.'

Monroe hadn't finished. This complicated jigsaw puzzle of intrigue still had a piece missing. 'Lekarev, why are these memos now so vital to the Soviet Union?'

'Khrushchev wants to embarrass America, to show the lengths to which the American government will go to achieve world domination. There is a summit coming up between Khrushchev and

Lyndon Johnson, and top of the US agenda is the subject of our tanks in Czechoslovakia. Eastern Europe is our sphere of influence, not Lyndon Johnson's. At the appropriate time, and in full view of the world's television cameras and press, Khrushchev will wave the Atlee memos in his hand as an example of how America had wanted to start World War Three in 1948. Copies will be provided to every member of the Security Council and each UN delegate, and to the world's press. Johnson will be acutely embarrassed.'

'All pointless now. Your own little escapade has been foiled.'

'There are no victors in this strange place today. I think that what we have just read must forever remain a secret between us. We have shared too much and there may be danger if we ever disclose that we knew the truth. I would not like to inform Barkovsky that much of what he obtained from his London agents was probably British disinformation. Nor would I like to be the KGB officer who now has to disappoint Nikita Khrushchev.'

Monroe was also considering his options. There were indeed risks to disclosure. There was so little time. 'Did you know there were *two* memos?' he asked urgently.

'I thought there might be, given what Barkovsky told me last night. He was quite drunk.'

'Your "Agent D" must have lost his nerve not once, but twice. He took a hell of a risk doing what he did, but there is still the matter of his accomplice.'

'Accomplice?'

'A personal friend of the major's … yet there is now also the possibility, given our thinking, that this accomplice worked for a British intelligence organisation. He could have targeted the major, cultivating him with the promise of male affection. That would have been a good hook. This man, whoever he was, might have been the link – the disinformation channel – to the major, who had not the slightest idea he was being used. But how did you know the major hadn't returned the memos, or indeed burnt them?'

'There was that possibility, but the decision was made to take the chance that he hadn't. We knew he was alive, and where he lived, but after twenty years we felt that only Barkovsky stood any chance of finding them if they existed.'

The silence in the wood was being loudly disturbed. As both men moved off the millstone urgent words were exchanged; there was even a handshake. Moments later the MI5 officers came crashing through the trees. 'What's been happening?' cried out the senior man. 'Why didn't you contact us?'

'Sorry mate … did try, but the radio was useless – no signal. It took some time to locate our Russian, but I did eventually,' reported Monroe confidently. 'I finally found him with this package in his hand. He'd opened it before I grabbed it out of his hands and floored him. Sorry, but here it is.'

'Did he read what was in it?'

'Couldn't definitely confirm that, but I think I reached him before he could have.'

'Do *you* know what's inside?' asked the senior man suspiciously.

'Haven't a clue,' replied Monroe in a detached manner.

The MI5 officers exchanged glances. On the Bluebird's face there was only pain as the handcuffs bit into his skin. Monroe looked on as the Russian was frog-marched up the hill to join Barkovsky.

★

That evening Stanley Lekarev and Vladimir Barkovsky were escorted by MI5 officers to the departure gate in Terminal 1 at Heathrow. The specially chartered Aeroflot aircraft had been refuelled and was ready to receive its only passengers.

Monroe and Harry were in a pub, going over their Exmoor adventure. Monroe had said little on the train back to Paddington. On arrival, they had gone to Charles II Street to file their statements, Monroe's concluding that he had reached the Russian just moments before the MI5 birdwatchers arrived. Monroe had not been greatly surprised to hear that Special Branch had received a vituperative complaint from MI5 that he had wantonly disobeyed orders not to intercept the Russians. As in 1963, they were calling for his dismissal from the service. 'Monroe's a loose cannon!' spat the MI5 contact down the phone.

'I had no choice.' Monroe shrugged at his superintendent. 'Radio contact was non-existent. The MI5 guys were on the other side of the valley.' The superintendent smirked. It was always satisfying to put one over on MI5. 'Go and celebrate, you two, before the pubs close,' he said with satisfaction in his voice.

At Ryder Street that night a meeting had been hastily convened. The MI5 chief reported that there had been a positive conclusion to the episode: the Russians were about to be deported at any moment. Rennie, the head of MI6, probed further into the nature and content of the two documents found in Clicket. They were being assessed, came the measured reply. Eyebrows were raised all around the table but no time-scale was offered to suggest when the contents might be shared with other organisations.

Such MI5 obstinacy did not concern Rennie. He had read the report quickly handed to an MI6 officer at Paddington station when Harry Tate had gone to locate a public convenience. Monroe had long been cultivated by MI6. His potential as an officer was regularly assessed. The Leeds adventure had not been helpful, however, and plans they had had for Monroe had been put in abeyance.

On the train from Bristol, as Harry had snoozed, Monroe had written down the wording of both memos as he remembered it.

In the pub Monroe finished his pint. He had to go, he told Harry, despite the offer of another. Harry hadn't probed his colleague about what had taken place in the wood. He had his suspicions, but those were thoughts he would keep to himself. He had not noted in his report that Monroe had asked him not to immediately call the MI5 birdwatchers that Barkovsky was taken. Only after fifteen minutes – as long as he dared delay – had he used the radio. The intermittant signal had given Monroe another five minutes.

Monroe took a cab to the Athenaeum. The bar of the private members' club was empty, given the late hour, apart from the occupant of an armchair by the window. Monroe walked over.

'So Monroe, you finally bagged the Bluebird. Sit down, have a

brandy.' The voice was authoritative and fingers were clicked at a hovering waiter desperate to retire for the night. 'I understand you insisted on seeing me – a most unusual request from a member of Special Branch to the head of MI6, if I may say so. You said to my colleague that you had some ... loose ends to tie up?'

'I have, Sir. Thank you for allowing me the opportunity. I reported to my MI6 contact the substance of the two memos. Have you read my report?'

'I have, Monroe. Very scary stuff.'

'Would I be correct, Sir, if I ventured to suggest that your organisation had no prior knowledge of the two memos, even though they were sent by Menzies, the chief of MI6 at that time?'

Rennie pursed his lips in a thin smile. 'A perceptive question. You've signed the Official Secrets Act, Monroe. Woe betide you if you ever repeat what I'm about to tell you. Menzies was a maverick, Monroe. A bit like you really.'

'That's an unmerited reputation I have, Sir,' interjected Monroe.

Rennie took a sip of his brandy and continued. 'As you know, Monroe, I was a career diplomat at the Foreign Office before my appointment to MI6 this year. I understand from my new colleagues that at times under Menzies, until his retirement in 1953, it felt as if there were two MI6 organisations operating against each other without a common goal. Menzies had an inner coterie, an arrangement that caused friction; it was resented by those in the outer circle who rightly believed that they were on the fringe. During the war Menzies undermined the SOE to our eternal shame, running MI6 as his personal fiefdom. When SOE was up against it we stood back. Outrageous! After the war we needed real cohesion in the organisation, given we were building up our rings in the Eastern Bloc, but it often appeared we were a bunch of intelligence amateurs. Menzies was the fundamental cause of the hostility and bad blood in MI5 – it was a mad state of affairs for this country. To make matters worse, MI5 never forgave us for the Philby business. One of MI5's chief snoopers had suspected Philby for some time; we chose to ignore the warnings. But I digress, Monroe – that doesn't answer your question.

'You wanted to know about the documents. There had been only rumours, I understand, within the organisation about Harry Truman's plan to wipe out Russia and start World War Three, but Menzies knew of course, thanks to his own intelligence network of contacts in America. His secretary must have typed up these memos to Atlee, and the copies for the Minister of Defence, but we have nothing in our operational files. If there were file copies Menzies kept them in his personal safe that no one ever had access to. They were probably with any files he had about MI6 contacts with Himmler. In early 1945 it was Menzies who instigated direct contact with a number of Hitler's henchmen, including Himmler, in an abortive plan to bring down Hitler. When Menzies retired he emptied out his safe and, at his home in Gloucester, burnt the lot, destroying the only record of much of the really secret stuff that happened during the war. If there were operational copies of the Atlee memos you found in Clicket they would have been destroyed. Menzies died in May this year, incidentally. He won't be missed.'

'Sir, I have another question. Was "Agent D"...' Monroe's voice tailed away. The Bluebird had warned him about saying too much.

On the train back to London his mind had been spinning as he tried to unravel it all. The major had been a spy for the Russians – a key one for Stalin. MI5 had a file to prove he was. But could he have been an unwitting pawn in MI6's Double X game during the war and early post-war years, that deliberately disseminated false information – to the Germans, the Russians, probably even the Americans? That little gem had been given to him by a newspaper journalist he had come to trust in recent years. Perhaps the major's accomplice at the Ministry of Defence was a member of this shadowy team?

Monroe's mind was racing. Why had the head of Britain's Secret Intelligence Services acceded to the request to see him? Rennie was not new to the murky world of disinformation. The man was a real pro. At the Foreign Office one of his past roles had been to head the notorious Information Research Department which regularly disseminated misleading material – even lies – to Fleet Street, the BBC and the foreign media. This diplomat would fit into MI6 very well, Monroe surmised.

'Monroe?'

Don't be stupid Monroe, reflected the Special Branch officer. Don't throw everything away now. Keep your mouth shut.

After the long pause he stuttered. 'Won't MI5 be giving you copies of the memos now they have them?'

'I doubt it, Monroe. Have we come to the end of your "loose ends" now?'

'There is something else, Sir. The Bluebird told me something in Clicket, moments before MI5 arrived. He thrust a piece of paper into my hand with a name on it, but he warned me to be careful how I handled it.'

Rennie ordered refills. Monroe handed over the name.

'Did he say anything else?' enquired Rennie, casually.

'He insisted I give the name only to someone I could trust. Lekarev said the man had been an agent for Moscow for years but had become a nuisance. Before he left Moscow Lekarev was instructed to suggest somehow to the British that the KGB was prepared to give him up. I happened to be the channel.'

'You've already checked out the name I suppose?'

'Of course, Sir. You'd have expected me to, wouldn't you?'

'The KGB never burn their agents. Why should they do so in this case?'

'We were in such a hurry in Clicket I didn't have time to ask, but I do know that it's the name of a Rear Admiral in the British Navy who sits on important committees in Washington that discuss US and British nuclear capabilities,' replied Monroe gravely.

Monroe felt Rennie's searching eyes boring into him. 'Careful, Monroe,' he warned.

'I have a request, Sir.'

'Yes?'

'If you do investigate the Rear Admiral, Sir, you will need a good birdwatcher. Can I apply?'

'I think we're done, Monroe,' responded Rennie, choosing to ignore the question.

Monroe immediately regretted his cockiness and stood up to leave, shaking the outstretched hand.

As he walked towards the door, past the yawning waiter, a voice from the armchair boomed loudly: 'Did you enjoy meeting your nemesis?'

'I did, Sir.'

'Enthusiasm is particularly winning,' said the voice, as an arm was raised again for the waiter.

'Monroe ... before you go.'

'Yes, Sir?'

'What did you *really* discover about "Agent D"?'

Monroe stood in the doorway, stunned. The wily old professional knew!

'Only what I have reported, Sir.'

Monroe left the Athenaeum. Like the waiter, he was dog-tired. Sleep would soon overwhelm him.

*

The letter could not have come at a more appropriate time. That very morning Monroe was due at Heathrow for another shift. With immediate effect, he read, he had been transferred to MI6 to report to a new special team, where his unique skills would be fully utilised.

*

Back in Moscow the Bluebird had been given promotion. For Vladimir Barkovsky there was only failure. He was overlooked for promotion to general, the appropriate rank for a man who managed a KGB department that controlled networks of spies in every NATO capital. Khrushchev had taken Barkovsky personally to task over his failure to claim the documents that could have enlivened his vitriolic encounter with Lyndon Johnson over Russian tanks in Prague.

The Bluebird had enjoyed his encounter with James Monroe. As he celebrated his promotion to major with fellow officers in the KGB club in the Lubyanka he wondered whether he would again cross paths with James Monroe.

∿

## The Bluebird

In 2008 the Bluebird celebrated fifty years in working for the Russian Intelligence Services. He now lectures on British Intelligence at the FSB Academy [the FSB is the successor to the KGB] and each year he runs a course for young intelligence officers from countries who maintain strong intelligence links with Russia. The Bluebird is recognised as one of the finest tennis players the KGB ever had in its ranks.

*On one occasion at a garden party in Moscow, hosted by the late Victor Louis, the Moscow representative of the newspaper mogul Lord Rothermere and a good friend of Robert Maxwell, the Bluebird played tennis with an MI6 officer, who was head of Moscow station, and who would many years later head Britain's Joint Intelligence Committee and become MI6's director. In the course of his MI6 career there would be many successes and some failures including agreeing to the preparation of a document that would take his country to war. The KGB nicknamed this officer 'Red'.*

In 2005, the Bluebird visited London, the first time for many years. He fondly remembers his postgraduate days at Leeds University.

## Colonel Vladimir Barkovsky

He would work for the Russian Intelligence Services right up to his death in March 2003. As the writer of the operational history of the KGB in the twilight of his career – an account for internal readership only and unfinished at the time of his death – he would enjoy unparalleled access to documents and secrets. Barkovsky was one of the KGB's greatest spymasters with his name  carved into the commemorative stone in the KGB History Room in the Lubyanka, an extremely rare recognition. He was never promoted to General, much to his dismay.

## Agent D

The identity of this agent for the Russian Intelligence Services has never been disclosed, but he was strategically-placed for the Soviets where he had access to the most confidential material, including Churchill's talks to senior German officers at the Vatican in September 1944 in a bid to engineer the downfall of Hitler and a German surrender.

## The Rear Admiral

For many years this senior officer provided military secrets to the Russian Intelligence Services. During the Cold War he was the top agent for Moscow in Britain and for some time was seconded to Washington. He was uncovered and ordered to retire from public service but was never prosecuted, using the legal system to guard against any leakage of his name.

## The documents

The ciphers of two documents relating to *Operation Chevalier* and *Operation Fleetwood* transmitted from the Russian Embassy in London in 1948 do exist in the operational archives of the KGB. They have never been publicly released, nor have any American or British documents relating to this episode which relate to the onset of World War Three.

# The Liberator

LOCAL HEROISM – A TRUE ACCOUNT

BY ALL ACCOUNTS October 29, 1942 was a filthy day. It was cold and heavy rain clouds obscured much of Bossington Hill, the landmark that dominates to the north of Porlock, Exmoor. In Porlock the war had brought the community ever closer together. Invariably, people made do.

On October 26 the Ministry of Food had again decreased the milk ration. The allowance was cut to two and a half pints a week for adults, though pregnant women would receive an extra pint a day. Confectioners, too, had new regulations. Only one layer of jam or chocolate was allowed on cakes.

Porlock had three ironmongers, three garages, three banks, two bakers, two shoe shops, five tailors and a fishmonger. In the fields, tractors were scarce, as was fuel. In Porlock Weir, the coal-boat *Democrat* at regular intervals brought in its full load of 98 tons, the locals helping with the unloading. In the harbour only registered fishing boats were allowed to fish, mostly for herring. Often the local farmers would come by and collect what was left of the catch to use as fertilizer on the fields. One boat at the Weir had already left its mark on the war. *Glenmorag* had been used in the evacuation of the troops at Dunkirk. Out in the Bristol Channel large vessels carefully steered their way, often at night, to Barry and Bristol with essential cargoes. Hidden beneath the waves, however, the enemy lurked. Many years after the war a former U-boat commander visited Porlock and told fascinated residents that his U-boat used to surface close to Culbone at night. His men would row to the shore in a dinghy to collect fresh water from a waterfall in a hollow near Glenthorne, the mysterious-looking early Victorian mansion set on the coast. Glenthorne had been owned by a German classics scholar called Hoffmeister, who to inherit the estate had changed his name to William Halliday.

Some two hundred miles south-east of Porlock, at the huge airfield at Holmsley South, in the New Forest in Hampshire, operated jointly by the RAF and the USAAF, the weather on October 29 was no better. The RAF and USAAF crews were being briefed on their missions for the day. A Liberator bomber with its twelve-man crew, attached to the 330th Bombardment Squadron, part of the USAAF 93rd Bombing Group but under the command of RAF Coastal Command, took off into the gloom at 7.20am.

Piloted by Captain William Williams Jr, who was usually based at the US airfield in Alconbury, this heavily armoured aircraft fitted with extra fuel tanks headed south to the Bay of Biscay on a secret mission to photograph U-boats making their way into the Mediterranean through the Straits of Gibraltar. Williams was an experienced pilot with 588 flying hours, of which 376 had been in Liberators. In the past three months he had also flown Westland-Lysanders, an aircraft in regular use for special operations.

The mission should have lasted eight hours ten minutes. However at 11.30am Williams decided to abort as the cloud ceiling was very low, averaging 400-900 feet, and flying continuously in cloud had badly buffeted the plane.

With bad weather still affecting Southern England, the Liberator was soon in trouble as the pilot and navigator attempted to find Holmsley. Hopelessly lost over the Bristol Channel, it circled Bossington Hill before clipping it, and crash-landed in the reed beds in Porlock Marsh at approximately 2.30pm.

There was one survivor, Staff Sgt. Herbert B. Thorpe.

*'After turning around, we flew for three hours before sighting land, and I heard Lt. Simpson, our Navigator, call on the interphone to tell Captain Williams that he was completely lost. Our maximum altitude at any time was 2,000 feet, all the rest of the time we were trying to fly*

*contact,*' Thorpe wrote later in his statement to the US aircraft accident committee.

'*Shortly after Lt. Simpson said he was lost,*' continued Thorpe, '*we sighted a point of land and circled it several times. After circling the point of land we moved up the coast with the land on the right and the water on the left. About ten minutes later we circled another point of land and then moved on. I was standing at the waist window, bracing myself against a gun-mount. Three of the others in the back end of the plane were lying on the floor asleep. Lt. Reiss (an extra pilot with us) had just come back before this to assure us that everything was alright. I assumed that we were in contact with a ground station. A few minutes later a large hill loomed up ahead. We made a steep climbing turn to the right with greatly increased power but suddenly we struck a downdraft of air. The plane straightened out but we continued downward. We struck the ground, bounced into the air and came down again, at which time I lost consciousness. When I regained consciousness I found myself in the place where our lower turret used to be. When I revived a nurse and some British soldiers were trying to prise me out and they just kept trying to calm me even though I was trying to tell them to help the others before me.'*

The inhabitants of Porlock had seen the Liberator in difficulty. Schoolchildren, including Ben Hammett, who still lives in the area, had seen it fly low over the village, obviously in trouble, and watched in the playground as the undercarriage came away to fall into Sparkhayes Lane, before the aircraft crashed in the reed beds burying itself into the soft ground. It didn't catch fire.

Those who were able ran to help the stricken aircrew. District Nurse Bragg, a tiny woman who lived in a bungalow close to Porlock Weir, struggled in the long reeds. She was physically picked up by Cecil Westcott, the fishmonger, and carried to the crash site. The soldiers of the Home Guard, mainly young farmers who trained on Sunday mornings, were quickly on the scene. Dr Forster, the village GP, a charismatic man who was known as a fast driver along the Porlock roads, grabbed his medical bag and joined in the chase. He and Nurse Bragg, with the help of the soldiers, gently manoeuvred Thorpe out of the turret. Albert Upstone, the ironmonger and a former navy man, and Frank Glanville, the local postman, climbed aboard the broken aircraft but the other crew members lay dead or dying. Ben Hammett's father, a veteran of the Battle of the Somme in World War One, who had been in charge of six ambulances at the

Front, had seen the crash while working in the garden of Chapel Knapp at Porlock Weir. A chauffeur and handyman to the owner, Mr Stilman, a former tea planter from Ceylon, Hammett downed his tools and ran as fast as he could along the stony beach to the reed beds to help the US airmen.

Crew error caused the crash, according to the official report that was kept secret for decades. One wartime British Liberator pilot told me that the Americans would not have been familiar at that time with the British system of QDMs, a network of signal transmissions used to guide aircraft safely home to their bases after missions. That was confirmed in the accident report: '*The weather was the predominant cause. There was restricted visibility, low ceiling and continuous rain over Southern England and in the patrol area throughout the entire period. The radio operator had not sufficient experience in RAF Coastal Command procedures. The pilot made an error of judgement in not flying at a higher altitude when it was definitely determined that he was lost.*' The report concluded that all pilots, navigators and radio operators should be thoroughly instructed in British radio signals and all crew members educated in fastening safety belts on take-off and landing.

In the US, the crash was widely reported in the press. Winston-Salem mourned the death of the newly-married Lt. Simpson, the first army officer in the town officially reported killed in action in World War Two.

A memorial was erected at Porlock Marsh, partly funded by a $100 USAAF donation. It included a plaque commemorating the dead, made by Frank Glanville out of metal from the crashed aircraft. Unfortunately there were some errors in the names of the dead, but this was not unusual on the high number of memorials erected throughout the country immediately after the war as records were not always perfect. One crew member was simply mentioned on the plaque as '*And one unknown*'.

A new plaque was engraved in 2003, to accompany the old one, with the full and correct names of all the dead. More than sixty years after the crash the name of the '*one unknown*' has finally been added to the list: he was Sgt. Stephen Prekel. Also on the new plaque is the name of the lone survivor, Staff Sgt. H.E. Thorpe. He never forgot the debt he owed to the villagers of Porlock and he often corresponded with Dr Forster.

*

Porlock and Holmsley South were, unfortunately, again to collide. On June 11, 1943 a Halifax belonging to 295 Squadron RAF took off from the Hampshire airfield. In May that year the squadron had begun to train Halifax crews to ferry gliders to North Africa as part of 'Operation Torch' in early August. The Halifax crashed into Ashley Combe, just behind Porlock Weir, narrowly missing Ashley Combe House (which has since been demolished). Four crew members were killed. Incredibly the pilot, Pilot Officer Basil Lawrence Thomkins, and the Flight Engineer, Sgt. Edward James Rogers, survived the inferno that followed the crash. A memorial is built into the side of the combe in the woods and can be reached via a walk from the Toll House.

Porlock and the surrounding area has a poor record for aircraft disasters. In addition to the Liberator and Halifax crashes, a German Junkers-88 crash-landed near the beach at West Porlock on September 27, 1940. The rear gunner, Wilhelm Reuhl, is buried in the churchyard of St Dubricus in Porlock, near the entrance to the cemetery, and his grave is regularly tended. No one knows who leaves the fresh flowers at the base of the cross.

A Bristol Blenheim belly-landed in a field at Porlock Bay on August 5, 1944 after an engine failure.

A de Havilland Vampire jet, lost in cloud, flew into high ground in cloud six miles south-west of Porlock on November 21, 1956.

A Chipmunk, also built by de Havilland, hit a hill in bad weather three miles south of Porlock on November 30, 1968.

*

These are the words on the new plaque on the memorial in Porlock Marsh. The memorial has now been moved to the coastal path, where it can be seen by the many who walk between Porlock, West Porlock and Porlock Weir.

*A Liberator, type B-24D, No. 41-23712, attached to the 330th Bombardment Squadron, 93rd Bombing Group of the American Army Air Force and based at Holmsley South airfield in the New Forest, Hampshire, took off at 07.20 on October 29, 1942 with a crew of 12 on an operational U-boat patrol mission over the Bay of Biscay. The aircraft turned around at 11.30 but three hours later, due to heavy rain and poor visibility, the aircraft clipped Bossington Hill and crashed into the marsh at Porlock not far from this memorial.*

*The dead:*
*Captain William J. Williams, II – pilot*
*First Lt. Lynn C. Riess, Jr. – co-pilot*
*First Lt. Joseph G. Simpson – navigator*
*Second Lt. Thomas W. Lewis*
*Second Lt. Charles G. Sorrell*
*Tech. Sgt. Walter D. Uffleman*
*Staff Sgt. James DeMuzio*
*Sgt. Stephen Prekel*
*Staff Sgt. Stephen V. DeMaroney*
*Staff Sgt. Earl R. Purdy*
*Act. Sgt. J.J. Odell*

*Staff Sgt. H.E. Thorpe was the sole survivor*

~

I have taken the details of the Porlock Marsh accident from US military aircraft accident reports, a copy of which I provided to Porlock museum.

This account was first published in *The Exmoor Review*, 2005 edition, Vol. 46, under the title 'Aircrews remembered 60 years on', pp.52-55.